Praise for *The Apoptotic Era*

"A.G. Valentine's ironically epic novella, *The Apoptotic Era*, about the shrouded history of a spellbinding, reviled, out-of-print book (about self-cannibalism, no less) is many things—a literary punk, an evolutionary lament, an ideological forensic, a love letter to book love and also—again, ironically—an intricately extended metaphor for the post-human mess we're now in, delivered with furious intelligence and wry humor. I've never read anything quite like it. Nor can I say what, precisely, it's about, not because it's inscrutable but because, like a prism, it shoots off interpretations in every direction, each one colorful and mesmerizing as the next. This novella's literary forebears might be Kafka, Pynchon, and Borges, yet it is completely its own beast—a bawdy, brainy artifact discovered at the algorithmic nexus of progress & collapse. I'm rather in awe of it."
—Rick Levin, author of *OFF ROUTE*

"Set in the chaotic years between Y2K and a near future of hyper-commodification, *The Apoptotic Era* follows dozens of characters sutured together through the messy stitches of their proximity to a mysterious book with an uncanny trail of bodies. With ankle-breaking turns, A.G. Valentine whips us back and forth between white knuckle suspense, lowing disquiet, and macabre hilarity. A must-read for a generation who may still not realize, all our lives, we've been the snake mindlessly gobbling our own tails."
—Armin Tolentino, Clark County Poet Laureate, 2021-2023

"A haunting meditation on loss, obscurity, and the strange afterlives of forgotten books, A.G. Valentine's debut, *The Apoptotic Era*, is a dazzlingly original novella that blurs the line between literary history and fiction. Through a kaleidoscopic narrative that traces the fate of a maligned, nearly vanished novel and its mysterious author, A.G. Valentine explores the ways stories persist—through errors, accidents, and the eccentric lives of their readers. At once darkly comic and deeply poignant, this book is a love letter to literary oddities; the secret histories left behind."
—Summer Stewart, publisher of UNSOLICITED PRESS

"Maze-like and spiraling, the very structure of this novella serves to express one of its core components: the feeling of having our collective experiences dissected and separated by the oppressive, governing forces of our lives."
—Maureen Brown, Co-Editor-in-Chief of
  JELLY SQUID MAGAZINE

"An absurdist ride through satirical prose, haunting body horror, and weird meta fiction. Overall, I'm relieved I read this account instead of *Autosarcophagy*!"
—Stephanie Pearre, Acquiring Editor of
  RAW DOG SCREAMING PRESS

"Enraptured by A.G. Valentine's hauntingly clinical prose, which conceals a sardonic wit under layers of viscera, I read *The Apoptotic Era* in one sitting while consuming two 'Six Shooters' and fourteen mentholated cigarettes. It was no small horror to realize that I'd been chewing on my cuticle for the final twenty pages."
—Pierre Manchot, author of *THE LEAST OF 99 EVILS*

"A.G. Valentine's *The Apoptotic Era* is a taut, intelligent novella that will appeal to fans of Kurt Vonnegut and Thomas Bernhard. With razor-sharp prose and immersive, meticulously crafted world-building, it offers a narrative that is both tightly focused and intellectually expansive. If you love being overstimulated by the art you consume (or consumes you), then this is for you."
—Jordan Krall, author of *FALSE MAGIC KINGDOM* and *YOUR CITIES, YOUR TOMBS*

"A.G. Valentine's debut is full of linguistic playfulness & violence. Humor juxtaposes horror in this series of vignettes that compels rereading. The novella churns inward like an ouroboros, like a man with a hook for a hand who has gotten it caught in his own skull."
—Benjamin McPherson Ficklin, author of *THE WEST & A CYNICAL VIEW OF DYSTOPIAN AMERICA*

The Apoptotic Era

A Novella

A.G. Valentine

Thirty West
Publishing
❦❦❦
10 YEARS
2015-2025

ISBN-13: 979-8-9895422-9-1
Cover artwork and design by Jacob Tyler Henry
Edited by Caterina Alvarez
Interior sketches by Kristina Vassileva
Author photo by Patrick Newson
Printed in the U.S.A.

For more titles and inquiries, please visit:
www.thirtywestph.com

"When there is nothing left to burn,
you have to set yourself on fire."

—Douglas Campbell / Stars - *Your Ex-
Lover Is Dead*

The book contains four errors. First, on page 106, the text reads "budgeoned" instead of "bludgeoned." Second, on page 122, the text reads "siced" instead of "sliced." Third, on pages 246-247 (the foldout leaf at the book's exact midpoint), the kerning is misset such that instances of *rn* are printed as *m*, and instances of *cl* are printed as *d*, producing, among others, erroneous instances of the words *dick* and *bum* as featured in the sentence, "The bone emitted an ominous dick; the sizzling flesh was starting to bum." (This error houses multiple errors, but is nonetheless counted as a single error.) Fourth, on page 353, the text reads "sallow" instead of "swallow." In books perhaps with wider appeal, such errors are inconsequential—the first run sells through and a second run is ordered with the errors corrected. In books such as this one, critically panned from cover to cover, the errors become part of a wistful decline—they sit on their respective pages, bound in spines that remain uncracked, in boxes on shelves in whatever warehouse such objects occupy until the day they are gutted for parts. To that end, the publisher confirms that all unsold copies of the book's first run have been pulped; recycled into informational pamphlets about genital herpes for distribution in Bulgaria, which has the highest seroprevalence of herpes simplex in the European Union.

*****

Writing for *Gebrauchtes Magazin* in 2001, freelance journalist Helmut Baumann called the book a travesty: That this *verschissen* compendium came to be printed at all, he wrote, is an indication that the midsize press responsible has editors who either lack judgment or are captivated by the bizarre—a trait better suited to magazine editors.

***

While an exact count of intact copies cannot be conducted, it is safe to assume that at least one copy of the book exists in the Northwestern United States, on a crowded bookshelf belonging to eccentric physiology scholar and Portland revolutionary Dolores L. Bright, who at age 58 cited the book as follows in the bibliography of her fourth master's thesis: Fleischer, Johan. *Autosarcophagy.* Borschau Press, 1999. Hardback edition; missing dust jacket; concave lettering; creased spine; 488 intact pages, 4 pages separated from binding, free-floating or floating free, frequently fluttering out to the floor, occasionally replaced backward necessitating on-the-fly rotation; epigraph faded; dried bloodstain on the contents page.

***

When questioned about their decision to greenlight Fleischer's manuscript, former Borschau Press reader and prescriptives editor Syl Gomes becomes visibly upset. They decline to comment on their thought process, stating instead that the morning the manuscript crossed their desk—which was, at the time, a folding table supporting a calendar of affirmations for the year 1997, a Brother ML-300 electronic typewriter, a photograph of their bloodhound, Chuco, and four empty Diet Coke cans—there was construction on the street outside and one of the machines was angled in a way that the sunlight bounced off its surface, through the window, into their eyes and held there beaming in at their brain. They scooted their chair a foot to the left and started reading the manuscript, but by the time they reached the bottom of page one, either the sun or the machine had moved and the spotlight was there on their brain again, so they scooted their chair one foot to the left, read a page, felt the sunlight, scooted their chair, read a page, and so on, one foot at a time, one page at a time until they were pressed against the wall, straining to shield their eyes from the light that fanned zoetropically throughout the room.

***

On Friday, September 3rd, 1999, a week after the book went to press, a Nacex delivery van containing 35 copies of the first printing among its cargo, to be sold in a bookstore called Siguiente Gran Lectura in the Spanish town of Medina Del Campo, was lost when the driver, a recently divorced father of two named Raúl Sanz Basurto, took a left turn instead of a right at the intersection of Calle del Zapardiel and Respaldo de Lope de Vega and accelerated the wrong way into one-way traffic. As cars swerved to avoid the speeding van, Raúl Sanz Basurto closed his eyes and swung the steering wheel to the right, sending his vehicle up a curb, across a footpath and public greenway to crash through the railing above the Zapardiel river. Onlookers describing the scene to police said the van appeared momentarily amphibious before it sank. No mention was made of a surfacing driver. The van was recovered and the railing repaired at Nacex's expense, but the cargo was so waterlogged that no books could be salvaged. Raúl Sanz Basurto's body was not in the van, and hauntingly, despite searching the river extensively (jackstaying all 52 kilometers downstream of the accident), authorities were unable to locate his remains.

***

Interviewed for *Wank* in the year 2000, guerilla zine illustrator and acid-house DJ Martin "Skoptics" Skeeves called the book an influence, citing its visceral imagery as source material for several of his more gruesome illustrations, as well as fodder for some "wicked street art."

***

The book's cover was designed by Hannah Gates, a Welsh artist who went on to design album covers for several small-time metalcore acts during the genre's period en mode in and around Cardiff in the mid-2000s, and who found herself in the late '90s working at a design firm called Hargate Dunn in Dundee, Scotland, having graduated from the Edinburgh College of Art's design school in 1996. How Borschau began using Hargate Dunn for its cover designs was never made clear to Gates. Nevertheless, it transpired that she was assigned to read and accompany Fleischer's work visually. The cover depicts an empty lot on a gray afternoon; a place entirely devoid of life.

***

Little is known about the book's author beyond his name or nom de plume (Johan Fleischer), his correspondence address at the time of his submission to Borschau (a P.O. box in Pilsen, scrawled on the enclosed SASE, used to receive and respond to the acceptance letter, the galleys and final proofs of the book, through which three typos slipped, to say nothing of the kerning problems), his fascination with unsourced and oral histories, and the fact that on formal documents, he signed his first name with a double n (Johann) despite never making this correction—or expressing the desire to have this correction made—on either the *Autosarcophagy* manuscript or its eventual published pages. While the P.O. box places him in the Czech Republic and his name appears German or Austrian, there is no indication that Fleischer speaks any language other than English; the book is in English, the submission was in English, all correspondence thereafter was in English. Those who care enough to wonder have theorized that Fleischer may be a fabrication; the alias of a celebrity, runaway, or other sought-after person, most prominently Salman Rushdie, who in 1997 was still in hiding and reputedly bouncing around the continent. That the book is so widely reviled lends credence to the expectation that Fleischer's identity will remain a mystery.

***

The first known copy of *Autosarcophagy* to reach North America arrived with Shane Billups, a high school exchange student who, in haste at running late to the airport, grabbed the book by mistake as he was packing to leave his host family's house in Lyon. Billups landed in Toronto Pearson Airport, Ontario, Canada, at 9:33 am on February 4th, 2000, five months after the book's initial distribution.

*****

The book presented itself to Dolores Bright as a bird of paradise presents to a prospective mate: with unique urgency, a vibrating presence that gripped her senses as she crossed the threshold of Wallace Books in southeast Portland's Sellwood neighborhood, seeking a copy of Knut Hamsun's *Hunger.* Before her search could begin, she became aware, as if by synesthesia, that a different title demanded her attention, buried like the proverbial princess pea amid the dozens of loosely alphabetized stacks that crowded the hardwood floors of Wallace Books in 2012. When at last she traced the source of this disturbance to the back corner of the miscellaneous section, the book felt like lightning in her hands; the used volume was missing its dust jacket, but a brief first-chapter perusal confirmed her suspicion: This book contained keys to her synapse locks; a desperate cautionary wisdom roiling within the writing's foundation, or the basement of the building that was *Autosarcophagy*, constructed by an author she'd never come across, whose name was German or perhaps Austrian, but whose command of the English language was strong enough that Bright's reading—or the reel of frames that whirred through her head as she read (the spell)—was rarely, if ever, broken, and although the chapter's content, a supposedly true account of a castaway who was forced to eat his own flesh to survive, made her nauseous, Bright believed this Fleischer was operating on the same wavelength as she, or which she had been the night her thesis topic sprouted in her head, as she lay in the bath surrounded by bubbles, tentatively masturbating to the memory of her grad-school lover—a mathematician with cornrows named Donald Foals, who died in a car crash in 1988.

∗∗∗

The owner of Siguiente Gran Lectura, a retired Hoover executive and expatriate from Canton, Ohio named Bill Jensen, awaited the preorder he'd placed for 35 copies of Borschau's next release—having had positive sell-through and ROI on their previous titles—for nearly two months before calling the company to check its status. He was told the driver had been in an accident, though no further specifics were offered. The replacement shipment was logged as en route. A month later he called again, wondering had his shop, which relied on new titles to break even each month inclusive of rent, utilities and further inventory, been somehow blacklisted, or otherwise forgotten, and if so, could he please procure an immediate refund so as not to mark a loss on this month's P&L, which he explained was growing tighter each year with the exponential growth of alternative entertainment sectors like premium cable, DVDs, video games and audiobooks—available now in both CD and cassette format at libraries, institutions he regarded as competitors, entrenched as he was in the growth mindset of undertaxed/underregulated hyper-capitalism fortified by the last three U.S presidential administrations and their respective congresses, and which he carried knee jerk into retirement, although savings-wise he was set for life, affording him the privilege of a passion-project. The Borschau rep sounded disinterested. They told him the shipment was marked en route. Jensen persisted. His business—and Borschau's reputation besides—was at stake. Hold please, the rep said, and following a subtle click, classical music filled the receiver.

***

Writing for *Нова Медицина* in 2009, medical analyst Petia Vassileva noted that over the four years since widespread distribution of literature regarding the transmissibility and prevention of herpes simplex type 2 began, Bulgaria's annual diagnosis rate fell 3.21% among adults aged 18-65, and a startling 8.34% among seniors. Demographically, Vassileva wrote, these trends are observable among Bulgarians and Turks, with numbers among the Romani population (likely underreported due to systemic societal exclusion barring adequate access to healthcare services) trending flat. She went on to praise the information campaign for its reach, and directed readers to voice their support for similar campaigns in the future.

***

The night janitor for the office building that housed Borschau Press in 1999 was a man named Peter Garminski, a bachelor with fifteen years' custodial experience and dreams of becoming a professional boxer, although his body was aging. Around the holidays that year, Garminski experienced a memorable uptick in plumbing issues—specifically clogged toilets—in the Borschau office, which took up two floors of a twelve-story building in Europapark, south-central Groningen, Netherlands. These issues were not isolated to any one toilet, nor specific to the gents or the ladies, and at first, Garminski speculated there must be a sickness going around, or else a new restaurant with massive portions where the Borschau staff were all eating lunch. The first blockages weren't particularly tough—a quick plunge job and the water spiraled—and so he continued his rounds, finishing fast so he and the nightwatchmen could begin their routine of drinking beer and watching old fights on the VHS player in the surveillance room. A week later, Garminski entered the women's restroom and found, to his dismay, every toilet clogged and overflowing. A quarter-inch of dirty water lapped against his boots. Specks of shit floated here and there. An orange tampon turned circles like a swan boat. Unlike the previous blockages, these obstructions did not dislodge easily. Stall by stall, Garminski plunged with all his might, the bowls acrid with backed-up excretions, waves rippling across the floor. At last, exhausted, he snapped on a rubber glove and reached into the toilet to relieve the congestion manually.

***

Officially—that is, according to Borschau's archives— the book's genre is history. However, in the handful of bookshops that carried *Autosarcophagy*, the title was shelved under the following sections: memoir, philosophy, nonfiction, fiction, historical nonfiction, horror, miscellaneous (as in the case of Wallace Books), human physiology, psychology, short stories, mental disorders, self-help, mystery, anatomy, folklore, food & drink, forensic medicine. Fleischer's opinions on this matter were never documented, and as stated, his identity and whereabouts are unknown.

***

Present at the one and only legislative hearing in which Fleischer's compendium was referenced on record were two seasonal contract workers: a stenographer named Ellen Börtsunder, who commuted by bus and dreamed (the nights she dreamed) in full sound, although she was born profoundly deaf and had never heard anything in waking life beyond a dull thalassic roar, and an interpreter named Valerie Stuart, who commuted on foot and was so tall she could stand anywhere at a concert and have an unobstructed view, if only she wasn't completely blind. As part of a short-lived program seeking contractors with disabilities to backfill open administrative positions (sometimes considered the spiritual predecessor to 2016's nationally-ratified *Bundesteilhabegesetz*) Börtsunder and Stuart were assigned cooperatively to backfill the live-transcription duties of a deceased White man whose employment record has since been expunged on account of his gross political leanings (inside sources confirm his name was Felix Hirsch, born 1919 in Idstein, Darmstadt, Hesse, active and vocal supporter of the Nazi party until the day he died), at roughly half the pay. Working together, the two women produced a transcript of a closed-door session in which the trend of new literature deemed excessively violent, sensationalistic, or otherwise unsuitable for young minds was examined by the *Bundesprüfstelle für jugendgefährdende Medien.* Central to the proceedings were anecdotes in which committee members and invited panelists discussed at length the ways words hurt them. While the book's title was not named explicitly, the transcript contains numerous mentions of people eating themselves without redemptive, educational or critical purpose, although it is possible that Börtsunder, in transcribing the session via Stuart, mistook the abundance of non sequitur opinions about where to eat lunch (half the committee wished to eat out, the other half had packed their own lunches) for references to one of the books in review, or that Stuart, in struggling to interpret the pinballing debate, missigned the concept of a self-packed meal and instead conveyed a meal of the self—an outrageous, albeit honest mistake. The session adjourned with six new books added to the register of adult-only works. *Autosarcophagy* was not among them. The program responsible for the Börtsunder-Stuart contract was defunded, and affiliation with the Bundestag severed.

***

On the materials list for her Portland State University course, *Human Physiology 443: Mindbody Interplay & Stimulus Response*, Professor Dolores Bright included Fleischer's book as a required text. In the run-up to the 2018 spring term, she received several emails from prospective students complaining that the book was unavailable in local bookstores, listed out of print with online retailers, and shipped from Europe when buying used, which entailed multiple weeks' shipping time at exorbitant cost. In response, Prof. Bright took her personal copy of *Autosarcophagy*—scarred as it was with markups and asterisks and notes-to-self and underlines and highlights and dog-eared pages—to the library computer lab and scanned the entire book page by page. In her eventual appearance before a university disciplinary committee, the deliberate duplication and distribution of copyrighted materials was cited as an example of Prof. Bright's disregard for university tenets, and entered into the official record as one supporting argument in favor of her immediate dismissal.

***

One morning while walking Chuco in the park west of their flat, Borschau reader and prescriptives editor Syl Gomes stepped in a puddle that was deeper than it appeared, and freezing water rushed into their trainer. It was late November and the park was empty. The puddle had a crust of ice. Using the playground fence for support, Gomes removed the waterlogged trainer and poured slush onto the pathway. They removed their sock and wiggled their toes. Chuco sat patiently watching his owner, who looped the dog's lead around their wrist and began to untie the trainer's laces. The dog padded forward and sniffed the spot where the water landed. He raised his tail. His hackles stood. What is it, boy? Gomes said. Chuco kept sniffing. He began to whimper as he locked onto the scent. Then, like a shot fired into the morning, Chuco charged forward with his lead pulled taut, nose-first against the ground, dragging his owner with one bare foot hopping across the spongy grass toward a small oak grove at the edge of the park. At the base of one particular tree, the dog stopped abruptly. Gomes was out of breath. Their bare foot was caked in mud, which rose above the hem of their pant leg, which was cold and wet against their shin, and their shoulder felt overextended (or hyperextended; torn or strained—any of these words, they knew, were suitable as substitutes were they editing their life on a page). Chuco continued to snuff and whimper, tail vertical, ticking like a metronome arm. The earth between the tree roots was barren and dark, and Gomes realized the absence of vegetation or even dead leaves looked unnatural, as though someone had slept there. Chuco's whimpers grew louder, rising in pitch as he honed in on the scent—what Gomes assumed was a scent, as opposed to some stimulus to a mysterious sixth sense—and then more prominent still; whining and growling, louder and louder until crows took off squawking from the naked branches overhead. What is it, Chuco? What have you found? At last, the growling came to a head and Chuco let out a single bark, punctuating the air in such a way that a ! flashed through Gomes' mind. They stood there breathing. The park was silent. Then, with all the strength of his forelegs, Chuco the Bloodhound started to dig.

***

As he stood listening to the hold music—which he believed to be a nocturne by Karl Hintz, the Bavarian cellist and composer who murdered (and reputedly drank blood from) three women in Regensburg in the 1890s— Bill Jensen, retired Hoover executive and transplant to the town of Medina Del Campo, owner of the independent bookshop Siguiente Gran Lectura, felt an abrupt tightness in his chest. A vacationing proctologist in search of a recently-published book called *Castillos Medievales de España* by Luis Monreal Tejada found Jensen splayed on the floor behind the register with no pulse, one hand clutching his heart, and the phone receiver near his head playing some sort of elevator music. The proctologist held the phone to her ear and listened, then pressed the hook switch and dialed 112. An ambulance came. Having been disconnected, the CSR at Borschau Press went on break. When the shipment arrived two weeks later, the courier found Siguiente Gran Lectura closed—its windows boarded, plastered with fliers for events in Madrid and a tangle of graffiti tags, among them a dung beetle with a Y2K sign, a host of decontextualized swear words, Atlético and Real Madrid tributes, condemnations of Prime Minister José María Aznar, and the Basque separatist slogan *Bietan jarrai.*

***

At age 102, slipping into the honey of death, beloved game show host and philanthropist Basil Small used his last words to whisper two things: First, there was a book in his house he believed to have cursed him, and second, people had been mispronouncing his name his entire life, including his family and the announcer on his show every night. It was actually pronounced Small. The loved ones at his bedside looked at each other in puzzlement, then held Small's hands as he drifted off.

***

Writing in to *The Portland State Vanguard* in 2021, Ursula Obianagha, a fourth-year physiology student minoring in folklore, penned a letter to the editor that called Professor Bright's dismissal—supposedly over the inclusion of unapproved, discredited and/or "dangerous" literature (that is, *censored* literature) in her syllabi—not only discriminatory, but retaliatory on the part of the University board of trustees, which, Obianagha wrote, is more interested in maintaining the stance that Black lives matter for capitalist clout than legitimately supporting its Black faculty and students, and which, given Professor Bright's ties to community organizers, activists and revolutionaries, including proponents of ANTIFA, Don't Shoot PDX, Willamette Action Collective and others, has made its allegiances clear with regard to the overfunding and escalating militarization of the PPD (and campus police, who are excessively armed with Glock 22 handguns and M26 tasers), the kidnapping via unmarked vans of several of its students by plain-clothes agents during protests last summer, and the morally regressive interests those agents represent. Obianagha went on to express that the Vice Chair in charge of Public Safety, Herbert Stouch, who presided over the disciplinary hearing, held a conflict of interest in that Prof. Bright was photographed exercising her right to protest outside his home in the southwest hills, where activists stood vigil demanding justice for LaToya Rice, a student who the aforementioned campus police tased repeatedly for the crime of being Black while walking home at dusk. Holding his finger on the trigger, Campus Safety Officer Ben Dunhill delivered a sustained charge of ~1200 volts into Rice with an M26 taser until she had a seizure. Rice was lying face down, defenseless, subdued by the initial shock, her laptop shattered on the bricks beside her. To date, Dunhill has not been arrested, fired, nor placed on administrative leave.

***

The book's library footprint is more or less incalculable because libraries have countless unofficial acquisition channels in the internet age, and fish those channels regularly. Official Borschau sales records between the book's publication date (August 27, 1999) and date of discontinuance (January 15, 2005) log zero purchases by public libraries. In Toronto, the copy smuggled transatlantically in Shane Billups' backpack was soon discovered for the fraud it was—masquerading as a hardback edition of Maupassant's *Mademoiselle Fifi* gifted to Billups by his host mother—and placed in a donation box that was dropped off at the City Hall branch of the

Toronto Public Library, where it gathered dust until early summer when a library-sponsored book sale at Larry Sefton Park saw the book placed on an unattended can-donation table with all the ghostwritten memoirs of B-listers, the manuals to declining computer technologies (*Floppy Disks: A User's Guide*), and editions of *The Guinness Book* from years past. The sale began at 9 am and drew passersby in fleeting clumps from the streetcar station up the block. By 1 pm, the book was gone. At this juncture, the piecemeal saga of the first copy of *Autosarcophagy* to reach North America is concluded—at least in this timeline—as no one has the slightest clue who bought the book, their destination, attitude, appearance, intentions, or whether they paid. Wherever that copy may be, it is identifiable by an oil stain on page 21, created shortly before the book's donation when Billups flipped through the early pages while eating a bag of all-dressed chips.

***

The catalyst for Borschau's relocation in the year 2000 was a biblioclastic incident involving a sectarian group called *De Voortgangsbewakers* (roughly translated as The Progress Keepers). Following the firings of three Borschau staff members over a spate of demonstrative book-flushings (about which Peter Garminski, night janitor for the building, complained explicitly, having fished by hand over forty coverless copies of *Autosarcophagy* from the office toilets in a three-month period), people in beige tunics and blood red eye masks began congregating in the parking lot on weekday mornings. They stood beneath a cloth banner that bore a sigil of a crippled left hand. While aesthetically creepy, the group's presence was physically unobtrusive, and at first, no calls were made with intent to expel them. As the days ticked on their numbers grew, most arriving by bike, but some by train and in automobiles that took parking spots from the building's staff, including Borschau editor-in-chief Mila Daalmans, who looked out at *De Voortgangsbewakers* from her second story office window, searching for—and finding—signs of familiarity in their mannerisms. Among them, she realized, was Christiaan Mulder, the recently-terminated nonfiction proofreader with whom Daalmans had orgasmed three times: first at the office millennium party, bent over the pine workbench in Peter Garminski's custodial closet with her panties pulled to one side; second, in the bed in her apartment, completely naked, her head thumping the maple headboard, and third in her office after hours, where Mulder licked her until she quivered, kneeling beneath her mahogany desk. The group as a whole worried Daalmans, but Mulder's presence exacerbated this anxiety. She worried about litigation. She worried about humiliation. She worried she might want to fuck him again. It started to rain. The masked people looked toward the heavens, but what they saw there was a mystery.

***

The book's epigraph reads, "You are what you eat," suggesting Fleischer has a sense of humor. The rest of the book has been called many things, but "funny" is not one of them. In 2026, a word cloud generator aggregating mentions across the web and metaverse (most hits appeared in archived scans of defunct print media) revealed English adjectives associating Fleischer's work:

Having discovered that the generator occasionally output nouns instead of adjectives, the person responsible for its programming, a Virtual Reality Systems Architect (VRSA) named Helen Tsang, became so depressed that she hurled herself from the fire escape of her twelfth-floor apartment. It was later determined that Tsang's mental health was questionable (a given), and neighbors on her floor, hypnotized by cold-war-era and subsequent hypercapitalist-era propaganda, believed she might be a communist operative. Neighbors also reported squelching noises late into the night. On her desk, beside a jar of yogurt whose microbiotic makeup matched that of the vaginal swab performed by forensic analysts at the behest of Tsang's ultra-conservative mother and father—which revealed Tsang had been cultivating food from her own body, far from having intercourse—detectives found a beat up copy of Fleischer's compendium open to a page so bruised with markups and equations and doodles of hands, the text was practically illegible.

***

While sick with a 39° temperature, Basil Small's assistant of 32 years, Rachael Watson, imagined herself as a felled tree in a mighty river, one of those wide fast rivers in America or Canada where lumbermen used to float unmilled timber and leap from log to log as they chaperoned the wood downstream, running them like treadmills through the meanders, and she imagined her skin was made of bark and smelled of vanilla before she was logged, and her roots stung, exposed as they were to the harsh air and frigid water, and her branches and leaves flailed behind her like ribbons tied to an AC vent. In the darkness of her bedroom where she writhed and sweated and shivered and groaned, Watson perceived the presence of a circular saw, its teeth slicing air thick with desiccated sap and hot green tree pulp and blue collar sweat, and commingled there too—perhaps as a manifestation of the window she kept opening and closing as she vacillated between overheating and freezing—gulps of fresh air from the vast surviving forests beyond the log camp's perimeter, and the radius of its destructive operations. And the saw was whining as she moved toward it, and then it was screaming and she was screaming and the blade ate into her bark and her pulp, splitting her irreparably, and she stumbled out of bed and rushed to the bathroom with vomit rising into her throat, and when she squatted reflexively before the toilet her bowels expelled a fiery liquid, the stench of which was so sickening she puked until she dry heaved and her diaphragm spasmed like a bisected worm. Exhausted, she slumped down and rested her cheek on the toilet seat. Limp as paper. She panted and winced, gazed at the dark of the toilet bowl, her bile in the water; gazed and panted as a memory shook loose.

Something her boss said—was reported to have said—before he died. As she crawled to the bathtub and turned the blue tap, convinced she would either die in this bathroom or colonize the tub as a new species of woman, Rachael Watson made a mental note: *Find the book that cursed Mr. Small.*

***

The reception phone at *Dagblad Martinistad*—a newspaper that in 1999 had an approximate circulation of 9,500, mostly via outlets in Groningen's south side and red light district—rang an average of eighteen times per week in the months leading up to Y2K, having tripled in volume since the sports reporter, Jacob Stoepke, was found dead in his living room with a plastic bag over his head and his trousers down around his ankles, penis in hand, face macerated by a cloud of autolytic moisture caught inside the airtight hood. Not only did this autoerotic humiliation spark adventurous requests in the brothels along Nieuwstad, it also became a running joke among secondary schoolers, who found it amusing to call the front desk and ask what type of balls the sports writer was playing with when he died. Ironically, external coverage of Stoepke's death sparked more letters to the editor in one week than all his articles combined over a twelve-year career in athletic journalism. Furthermore, external coverage of Stopeke's death drew more readership in one week about *Dagblad Martinistad* than *Dagblad Martinistad* drew to its own pages in a calendar year. But after the initial flurry of calls requesting comments outside the paper's official statement—a heartfelt obituary on page 7 complete with a full-color photo of Stoepke wearing the FC Groningen green and white—most additional call volume came at the hands of pranksters. So when a tip came through that a local dog had unearthed a severed hand in a park near Ulgersmaborg, the paper's receptionist, Vera Hirsch, assumed the kids were at it again and hung up the phone without second thought.

***

With the dust cover included, the book weighs 1lb, 15.4 oz, which can also be formatted as 1.96 lbs or 31.4 oz, or converted to metric as 0.89 kg, 889.04 g, 889041 mg, or impractically as 0.00087 imperial tons, 0.00089 metric tonnes, 0.00098 U.S. tons, or for those familiar with British bathroom scales, 0.14 stone. For those requiring comparative examples to contextualize these measurements, the book weighs roughly the same as 1 Malayan flying fox, 29 athletic socks, 889 paperclips, or 20% of an adult house cat. Dimensionally, the book measures 9.5 inches long, 6.5 inches wide, and 1.9 inches deep. Anecdotal evidence suggests the book's conversion to a Solander Case is viable, although upon hollowing the book, the craftsperson responsible could expect to fit only a few small, sentimental trinkets, a half-ingested powder-drug stash, or a piece of human anatomy subject to the respective soft-tissue morphology of the mummification process, which entails a soft-tissue shrinkage rate of ~90% among ice mummies, and still higher among appendages mummified in warm climates.

***

Packing up her office in the SRTC sub-basement, outgoing physiology professor Dolores L. Bright began counting breaths to keep her composure, furious as she was with her situation—terminated without appeal, humiliated via email in front of her colleagues, and saddled now with the deliberate fuck-you that was her final security escort: Officer Ben Dunhill stood in the doorway watching Dolores pack. He smelled of cigarettes and Axe body spray. She breathed and counted: *Inhale one, exhale two, inhale three, exhale four.* As she plucked the books from the shelf above her desk, she thought about the molecules in the air around her, the deconstruction of molecules in the processing chambers of Dunhill's body; waste products fired in her direction, twining themselves with her microbiome, permeating her face mask and colonizing her passageways. I'm ready, she told him, and Dunhill stood aside as she passed. In the echoing stairwell, she listened to his breathing as he stalked behind her; the breathing of a predator or the squealing lung inside a predator—something massive and predatory and pervasive such that she already knew its breath, had felt its breath all her life like a cloud draped over a devastated butte. At Market Street, she didn't look back. She boarded the MAX and rode east across the river. Home in her studio on 9th and Belmont she poured a shot of Absolut and counted breaths while the city outside seemed to bloat with an inescapable gas; a putrid malevolence codified in protective corruption, in donor networks and quid pro quos, the relentless solicitation of shiny morsels; doomed, increasingly, to consume themselves. With Professor Bright's passing (because professionally she was good as dead), so too passed the book's last chance to proliferate via an institute of higher learning. In the years to come, no former students reached out about the book. No arrangements were made to acquire a copy for the PSU library. The memory of Dolores Bright's class burned off, and with it the memory of her strange syllabus and the endangered literary obscura at its center.

***

A 2007 episode of the French serial drama *La Vie Née Belle* marks the book's only known television appearance. While infiltrating the mafia in an operation aimed at ensnaring a high-profile Lyon kingpin, the cop character Gerard Mimieux—played at the time by Gerard Herman, whose career went nowhere following his last appearance on the show in 2009—finds himself and his husband, Thomas Clement, kidnapped and awaiting death or torture in a room with a bookshelf. In the eleventh hour, when all hope seems lost, their captor—the kingpin—is murdered suddenly by his own daughter, who shoots him in cold blood. She has fallen in love with Gerard Mimieux, who, despite being married, has recently slept with her to get closer to his mark. The book appears during the patricidal scene—a gray brick on the shelf in the background, visible for perhaps one second, no more than two, though if somebody were to pause and zoom in, they could decipher the title printed on the spine; a semi-legible blur in the midst of a scene whose pivotal moment rests with an actress named Margaux Lafaile, whose face is fraught with sorrow and determination as she levels a pistol at her make-believe father.

***

Speaking into an Olympus S922 micro-cassette recorder, the medical examiner assigned to Politiebureau Groningen case #124294-B (which was known around the coroner's office as *De Handjob*)—a man named Jaan Peltz with degrees in forensic biology and criminology from the University of Amsterdam and King's College London respectively, and whose medical residencies took place at Charité-Universitätsmedizin Berlin—reported that the hand unearthed in Ulgersmaborg was indeed human, a left hand with approximately five centimeters of forearm attached, confirmations that perhaps served to waste precious tape, but which were true, and to the matter of the bite marks on the inner-wrist, some so deep that the trapezium and scaphoid bones as well as the pollicis longus tendon were visible beneath the chewed flesh, Peltz noted that not only were the wounds inflicted by human teeth, the angle at which the teeth sunk in suggested the bites were self-inflicted. In fact, Peltz said, the word "bites" is inadequate to describe the tenacity with which human teeth tore into this hand. By his estimate, and according to the presence of nascent active decay, the hand had been separated from its owner no more than a week. He went on to note that the complexion was brown, type IV on the Fitzpatrick scale, like that of a working-class Spaniard, again wasting tape, and concluded: This hand has been partially cannibalized by its host and should be cryogenically retained until the crime with which it corresponds is made apparent. That night, having nodded off to a documentary about emperor penguins, Peltz dreamed about the partially eaten hand and the angle of the teeth and he dreamed about a plughole in IJsselmeer and a network of flumes beneath the earth's crust and he dreamed there were lumps of wet flesh on his tongue, lumps he had to chew and swallow despite the fact he knew they were human; despite the fact they were parts of himself. On the TV screen, the penguins marched while a blizzard raged, and they bowed their heads as they persevered.

***

Rachael Watson contacted Basil Small's youngest son, Anthony, via one of the most outmoded means of correspondence available in 2043: a landline telephone connected to the emergency grid for use in case of apocalyptic events stemming from climate change, further mutations of COVID-19, the brutal machinations of hyper-capitalism's implosive endgame, a weaponized EMP or other cyberwar systems-collapse scenario, or else mass introitus into the metaverse leaving the outside world to ruin, the latter of which had been underway since the early 2030s, as the prospect of a metaverse-based social life, job market and lack of lucrative external alternatives attracted urbanite children whose souls—and by extension their personhoods, their biologies, their physiologies, their sexualities—were ensnared and digitized and placed on sale as part of a colossal algorithmic advertising trap the moment they sculpted their avatars. Having undergone a renaissance among aging Gen X hipsters and pining middle-aged millennials, to say nothing of the baby boomers clinging on for dear life, letters sent via Royal Mail actually overtook landline phone usage for two weeks in the winter of 2039, with the number-one means of interpersonal correspondence being Virtual Reality hangouts for the seventh year in a row. When she asked Anthony—who answered his cell with a brusque "Yeah?"— what his father actually said on his deathbed, Anthony responded that he couldn't remember. Also, he was incredibly busy and didn't have time to chinwag with Dad's ex-employees, so what exactly did she need? Rachael Watson explained her recent illness and the inexplicable redemptive determination that struck her as she swirled in a puddle of her own excrement. She asked Anthony if he knew to which book Mr. Small was referring. He didn't. But there's a mountain of shite needs sorted here, love. (He might have said love, or missus, or babe, or bruv. His voice was coming at a thousand miles an hour, the words interspersed with compulsive sniffing). Come and have a rummage if it means that much. After they hung up, Watson looked out her window and thought about Basil, about his hands and his voice and the sandpaper stubble that gave definition to his jawline, and she thought about all those nights in the twenties, cool summer nights where they'd sit and talk and neck and footsie, watching the lights pulsate on the Thames.

***

As Borschau editor-in-chief Mila Daalmans watched *De Voortgangsbewakers* from her second-story office window, she wondered how many knots it would take to lash herself to the prow of a ship. Raindrops beat the body-length glass. The sect members huddled together beneath their banner, which they held like a canopy over their heads, the mangled hand sigil signing menacingly up at the sky. Though she lost him briefly, it wasn't long before Daalmans caught sight of Mulder again. He was hunkered beside a woman with dirty-blonde hair and black lipstick. The customary blood red eye mask obscured the woman's features, but even so, Daalmans could tell she was beautiful. Certainly Mulder seemed to harbor some attraction, the way he kept brushing her forearm, the mouth below his eye mask a constant coy smile, working the blonde woman with the same moves he'd used on Daalmans in the lead up to their first utilitarian fuck—the preface, literarily speaking, to part one of their sexual trilogy. As she watched this familiar courtship play out, a venomous jealousy coursed through her, surprising her, and she turned away to face a desk strewn with backlogged correspondence from readers, retailers, former employees, current employees, journalists, and janitors. God, she thought, there is no god. In her deposition the following month, Daalmans told the property owner's counsel that she wasn't insane—her headaches and heart palpitations were symptoms of stress, nothing more. They're getting worse all the time, she said. Can't you see I've been through hell?

***

Although news of the hand's discovery was widespread, the fact that it had been auto-cannibalized broke slowly due to skepticism from national-level newspaper editors who did not wish to print hearsay (or second-hand hand news), but who were curious nonetheless and ordered phone calls to the Politiebureau Groningen to gather official statements. The official response was No Comment, which more or less confirmed it was true, but which was useless without another story to embed the No Comment within. This pushed the subject into slush for most national news outlets, who were busy reporting on Y2K panic and the Dutch government's promotion of antitrust-sheltered ISACs. The party responsible for leaking the forensic analysis remains protected under reporter's privilege, however it has been speculated that Jaan Peltz himself operated as a confidential source for a few local rags in 1999, among them *Dagblad Martinistad,* which fired Vera Hirsch for missing the original scoop and chased down this addendum as consolation—an addendum that Syl Gomes, having spread the relevant issue on their breakfast table, cut out with scissors and added to their scrapbook alongside *Algemeen Dagblad* and *Telegraaf* clippings about their dog's discovery. At the office that afternoon, having drunk a fourth can of Diet Coke during lunch, Gomes visited the restroom and saw, gazing into the toilet bowl, a torn book page floating in the water.

***

At 3:07 pm on Thursday, April 13th, 2000, union plumber Maxim Köhler was walking his nine-year-old daughter, Lara, home from school along Verlengde Meeuwerderweg, swatting the midges that had hatched on the pond and replaying a dream he'd had two nights prior in which Lara was trapped inside a car. It was a gold car with unbreakable windows and a complex locking mechanism unlike any he'd ever encountered, which required the use of his plumbing snake to unlock, and which ran the circumference of the vehicle three times between the chassis and shell, turning his snake into a boa constrictor. He woke up in a cold sweat, took a shower, ate a bowl of Brinta, took Lara to school, then went to unclog a university student's toilet. As they rounded the corner onto Lodewijkstraat, Lara Köhler looked up at her father, her hair and overalls sticky from a Mentos-and-Coke demonstration her teacher had performed at school, and for a long moment he loomed large enough to blot out the sun. Particles danced at the edges of his silhouette, multiplying in the muted brightness. Look, Papa! It's snowing! Lara stuck out her tongue to catch a flake, but the snowflakes evaded, darting away as though magnets repelled them (another school demonstration). Shaken into the present moment, 3:07 pm on Thursday, April 13th, 2000, Maxim Köhler looked about, impressions of the dream still etched on his vision. I don't think that's snow, he said. Lara stood there awaiting the flakes. At last one landed and her tongue recoiled. Her features scrunched as she pondered the taste. It's salty, she said. Ugh! She spat. *Walgelijk!*

***

First thing Monday morning—as though the caller were counting down the seconds—the wall phone in sub-basement 1F of the Politiebureau Groningen Centrum rang with a shriek. Cold-case evidence clerk Marilyn De Groot, hungover from a party the night before, winced as she picked up the receiver. *Ja,* she said. The voice on the other end was American. It made no attempt to speak Dutch at first, nor did it ask if De Groot spoke English. It simply talked; thick, almost buttery timbrations that slid into Marilyn's ear until, curtly, she interrupted the voice and told it she needed to boot up her system. Her head was pounding, but she couldn't help grinning as she logged the request in her tablet; a DNA sample from a twenty-two-year-old case, a famous case with a vulgar name. According to the database, the case was closed pending further evidence; marked with reference code 824, meaning its physical assets were available for use in scientific research. This is possible, she told the voice. Please email me your research credentials and timeline so we can arrange a slot for you to collect this sample. Two days later, the stairwell doors to sub-basement 1F opened to admit a woman in a pencil skirt, flats, and cardinal red silk blouse. After scanning her visitor pass and ensuring biometrics were in order, De Groot led the American into the locker. The overhead striplights buzzed and tinkled. Owing to its age, the case was packed deep in the cabinets on the far-back wall, amid a series of archives awaiting digitization. Marilyn located the evidence file, which listed a reference key to a cryogenic chamber in the biological repository, which was through a door with a security keypad. The repository was cramped, cold. The lights flickered. The American looked down at the floor, or at the walls or the rows of refrigerated blood samples in vials—

anywhere, it seemed, except the ceiling. Here we are, Marilyn said. They stopped in front of an opaque cylinder with a reference number matching the case file. A small button on top made it open with a hiss. Marilyn gasped. I don't understand, she said, checking and rechecking the reference. This is the right one. The hand should be here. At that moment, the American scientist hit the floor with a thud, and to Marilyn's horror, began convulsing.

***

Following her fourth appearance on British TV, French soap star Margaux Lafaile was photographed entering a candlelit restaurant called The Jade Fountain in Highbury with none other than longtime gameshow host Basil Small. According to the accompanying blurb, which was printed in the June 2014 issue of tillstand tabloid *Stars Blast*, the pair sat at a small, round table in the shadowy back-corner, leaned into one another, engaged in a conversation so thrilling it appeared that their own fame or semi-fame—that is, their effect on the atmosphere— seemed to elude them. The paparazzo responsible for snapping the photograph, a kidney pie enthusiast and West Ham supporter named Gareth Barnes who slept each night with his lager-filled belly pressed against his rigid wife, Tilly, who hadn't shagged Gareth (or anyone else) in four-and-a-half years, sold the scoop to *Stars Blast* for

£25. The part he left out in his recounting of the date was a mysterious exchange, between courses, over two matching gray hardback books, which Lafaile and Small held open between them.

***

As they bowed forward to examine the floating book page, a cough from the adjacent stall made Syl Gomes jump. Inside the adjacent stall was Christiaan Mulder, the nonfiction proofreader, who recently went to Spain for two weeks, and whose cough since returning had grown recognizable due to its persistence. The trip to Spain had an undetermined or at least undisclosed purpose, though most assumed it was a late holiday, and since his return, he'd been coughing like a cigarette smoker or an asthmatic smoker or an emphysemic smoker or a smoker of menthols. It was true that in Spain he'd smoked a few cigarettes, and shared a spliff with a girl in Marbella who worked the till at a video rental, and he'd slept with a different girl in Ronda, the birthplace of bullfighting, an hour's train north. Her profession was never made clear, although she ordered him to fuck her like a bull who'd pinned a matador, and so turning this over in his head two days later he concluded she must have been a tour guide. Then came a night in the middle of the trip—somewhere in the depths of the tunnel; that midpoint bend in the memory tunnel where the light at either end is extinguished—on which, having drunk two liters of cheap sangria with a barfly on Calle de San Lázaro, Mulder found himself lost in a network of alleys with only his backpack and two open beers he couldn't remember purchasing. The alleys were winding and filled with shadows. The smell of the Mediterranean pooled inside them. An hour passed, or some amount of time in which his heart kept beating and the cans in his hands lost half their weight. Perhaps it was simply a trick of the moonlight, but as he searched in vain for a way to the road, Mulder felt himself drifting in and out of consciousness; back and forth across the face of a dream. The more turns he made, the louder his heartbeat, the fainter the shuddering of downtown Marbella became, and it occurred that a centripetal force was acting upon him, drawing him into the heart of a maze—a maze shaped like a gigantic vulva—and with every step he was trekking back to the site of his birth. On the other side of the bend in the tunnel, having careened toward a halo of light, Mulder awakened in a hostel bed to a room encased in cytoplasm, a 37.5-degree fever and a throbbing pain in the tip of his cock. I've caught it, he thought. I've contracted Spanish flu. On the bedside table, which was just a wine crate set on end, he deciphered the shape of a hardback book; some gray brick he'd promised to read as a favor to a coworker. He buried his face in the sweat-drenched pillow and tried to recall the last passage he'd read—any passage of any book he'd ever read, any sensation in his brain or limbs or abdomen to dull the pain in the tip of his cock—fumbling his way back into the darkness.

***

Those speculating as to how the book appeared in Shane Billups' host family's home will be hard-pressed to guess the truth, and to report the truth plainly may be counterproductive, or at least distracting, as the truth imparts an unwarranted mysticism onto the book or the idea of the book as a tangible object, albeit one with an intangible aura of controversy and despair. All that can be said of winter '99 in Auvergne is that the nights were unusually stormy, and rumors—or more accurately urban myths—began to circulate that at midnight on new year's day, a sinkhole would appear at the confluence of the Rhône and the Saône, and the Presqu'île would be swallowed whole. In an address to local media, Mayor Raymond Barre (former prime minister with a track record of minimization when it came to the concerns of his working constituents, especially those in trade unions) spoke of the rumor as one might a maple seed helicoptering onto a city street: *C'est intéressant,* he said, *mais impuissant.*

***

Having seen her relatives off at the airport, relatives from Yangshizen who deemed her daughter's death an omen of misfortune, or a powder keg that could ignite itself at the slightest provocation—that is, in testing fate by sticking around in this city of high ledges and falling air conditioners (although she knew their distaste for the USA in general also played a part)—Lin Tsang, mother of the recently deceased VRSA Helen Tsang, rode home alone in a rideshare full of loose golf balls that rolled around on the floor at her feet, bouncing and darting as though she were a peg in a Galton board, a nuisance for which the driver apologized, but did nothing to rectify. He had music on the radio, too; European hyperpop that made her hair stand on end. She rolled down the window and tried not to cry. At home, she prepared a pot of jiaozi soup, which she thought of as her daughter's favorite, and stood in the kitchen and closed her eyes and allowed the steam to fill her lungs. On the backs of her eyelids, she saw a field of white irises, a gigantic rectangular field of white irises stretching toward an open horizon, and where the sky met the earth she saw a blood red sun, a taunting sun, a corona of confusion. She was still in the kitchen when her husband, Jinhai, came through the front door. More bullcrap, he announced, throwing his satchel on the bench in the entryway. These *gweilo* cops don't know what they're doing. Now they think it was crypto-related. Crypto? Lin asked. Yes, Jin said. Can you imagine? I can't see how this has anything to do with money. Lin ladled a steaming bowl of her soup. Can't we just eat dinner? she said. Yes, *Tiánxīn*, Jin said. But first thing tomorrow, we're going back down there and finding out what really happened. And I want to know the significance of that book. Eat, eat, Lin said. And they did.

***

Groningen's downtown shopping district, which fans outward from the Grote Markt—a historic plaza used annually, among other things, to commemorate the Netherlands' survival of its most metal year, the *Rampjaar*, 1672, in which the Dutch lynched and cannibalized their own prime minister—contained two craft shops in 1999. The first was a hobby store that thrived on revenue from model airplanes, battleships, and railway kits. The other, two blocks up and two over, did not sell model airplanes or ships, or in fact anything hobby-related, as the owner, a monobrowed widower named Willem van Tol who spent his nights woodworking and telling his dead partner's urn about life's myriad dissatisfactions, believed that crafts and the crafting of crafts was an artistic pursuit to be taken seriously. On Tuesday morning, December 21st, van Tol was taking inventory while listening to Karl Hintz' "Der Wald Des Todes" when four men in beige tunics entered his shop, tailed by a blonde woman. He nodded in greeting and continued his work. From his stool at the register he could see the whole shop, and as he worked his biro down a page of short SKUs—for example, he was running low on silver sequins, leather punches, tartan ribbon and hot glue sticks—van Tol kept an eye on the people in tunics, who he assumed to be monks, and raised his eyebrow when they gathered around the fabric spools in a conspiratorial formation, as though they were planning a robbery or heist, or as though they were players in an American sports film, or as though they were showing each other their privates, or as though they were conducting a seance. *Mag ik u helpen?* he asked. The people in tunics stopped their discussion. They seemed perturbed. The blonde woman shook her head at van Tol and pursed her lips as if to say, *Please don't ask again.* She was a slender woman with black lipstick and a cragged face, by no means beautiful, though not without character. Van Tol returned to his inventory, but he turned down the radio—using the climactic bars of "Der Wald Des Todes," which crescendoed to a violent forte, as an excuse to do so casually—and cocked his ear to their conversation.

***

Generating for a segment called *Sleutel Vergeten* in 2035, a Dutch multimodal large language model named *46-Robbens* aggregated what little information existed about *De Voortgangsbewakers* to form a retrospective profile. The group's intent, *46-Robbens* reported, was ill-defined. It had few tenets and did not operate under a centralized manifesto. As with most millenarian cults, especially those influenced by henotheistic forms of religious expression, The Progress Keepers were duped into radical action at the behest of a premier whose motives lay with financial, spiritual and/or sexual hegemonic gain (*droit du seigneur*). One key differentiator the AI reporter noted was that the group had a female leader. *46-Robbens'* objective function did not include the discernment of gender normatives, nor the stereotyping of its analytical subjects, however it saw fit to note this differentiator, indicating the leader's gender was anomalous enough, historically speaking, to warrant output.

***

Ninety minutes south of London, Basil Small's mansion stood like a false tooth in the blackened gum of a once-lush deciduous forest. Crows took flight from the circular driveway as Rachael Watson parked her E-ped and dropped its kickstand into the gravel. Using the spare key she cut years ago, she unlocked the front door and waited, listening. Anthony, although he was given power of attorney and ostensibly cared about disentangling and reorganizing his father's affairs, was not here (as evidenced by the vacant driveway), and per Basil's will, the housekeepers, gardeners, and cooks on staff had all been granted severance. This gave Watson free rein of the house, unbridled access to the chambers in which Basil kept his secrets; the chambers in which their affair played out, and other rooms Watson knew existed but never got a chance to behold—concealed chambers discoverable via eccentric mechanisms that Basil only ever mentioned in the absentminded afterglow of their lovemaking. While they split cigarettes and watched the smoke pool on the vaulted ceiling, Basil would mutter mysteriously to himself, "The trapdoor switch in the library needs grease," or, "The candelabra tunnel is dusty." After that he'd usually fall asleep, and Rachel would dress and draw the curtains and attend to the administrative priorities of the moment—dinner reservations or ghost correspondence or other minutiae within her purview—and when Basil awoke, their relationship reverted to its asexual origin: employer and employee, until next time. Standing in the grand foyer, the passage of time between then and now gripped Watson's limbs and racked her lengthwise. She understood with stunning clarity that even back then, before the illness and before the tears and before his erections started to soften, Basil's mind was beginning to fail him. The foyer was cluttered with boxes and flotsam, nascent preparations for an eventual estate sale, but otherwise looked as it always had—as it did the last time she hurried through it, the day their physical affair met its end to make room for a long-fingered nurse named Bex who was willing to tickle Basil's prostate, and Watson's heartache began crystallizing into something spiky and sparkly and cold; into something reminiscent of sudden sobriety; into something she'd grown to think of as unconditional love.

***

At 2:02 am on February 2nd, 1986, Dr. Robert Shankley, the surgeon on-call in the maternity wing of Eastlake General Hospital in Bellevue, WA, sank his scalpel into the belly of a deceased woman named Ronnie Foals and extracted from her womb a living child. Dr. Shankley looked at his watch and noted two minutes had elapsed between the mother's death and the infant's birth; statistically, a low probability of brain damage. The child was named Aaliyah, and her mother was buried two weeks later on a gray day like any other. Two months after her 2nd birthday, Aaliyah's father, Donald, having entrusted his daughter to an old White couple two houses down, attended a lecture hosted by UW's mathematics department entitled *The Born Body: Disciplinary Intersections in Physiology & Quantum Mechanics*, in hopes he might run into an old girlfriend named Dolores, whose mind he was certain could illuminate the universe, her brilliance unrivaled by the billion-year light-strength of long-dead stars (to say nothing of her ass), and whose work since graduation eluded him, but whose graduate research was historically congruous with the topic du jour. To his disappointment, Dolores did not attend the lecture. Her name appeared on a slide near the end, credited as an intern. Driving home across the 520 bridge, Foals' mind swam with concepts and memories: his mother's singing voice, the infinite mysteries of wave functions, the comparison of a living body to the Ship of Theseus (an analogy posited during the lecture with regard to apoptotic cell turnover—the natural, recurring process by which healthy cells die, are cannibalized via macrophages within their host organism and promptly replaced with identical successors—begging the question: *Are we really who we used to be?*), and he thought about Ronnie's hair on his cheek, Aaliyah's golden-sage colored eyes, Dolores' fingertips white with chalk, his own heart pounding in the darkness of his chest. But above all what he turned in his mind as he exited the freeway into downtown Bellevue was a postulation the lecturers referenced, a decoherence mechanism called quantum chronofractolysis, which theorized a wave function could exhibit reactions to self-wrought replications of itself—impressions shed, for lack of a better word, at key milestones within its predicted trajectory that could in turn be parsed into individual wave functions, and under specific conditions within the confines of their shared trajectories, each of these synecdochical wave functions could collide and interface with its counterparts, corrupting itself with itself infinitely within the bounds of itself to create a polydimensional, strobographic entity. The city lights seemed to fold into nothing. So lost in thought was Foals at that moment, the semi-truck didn't even register. At the intersection of 112th and Main, a spun-out long-hauler named Daryl Freidman slipped the red light and T-boned Foals at high speed. Two years later, emerging from the fog of her life's onset, Aaliyah Foals found herself in DHS custody, awaiting adoption in a state-sponsored foster home.

***

Wiping his mouth with his shirtsleeve, Christiaan Mulder felt as lost as ever on the floor beneath Mila Daalmans' desk. A wet spot shone on the leather chair between her thighs, which moments ago were vised so tightly to the sides of his head that he was plunged into temporary deafness. Reclining, red-faced, Daalmans bunched her blouse at her chest and exhaled. Mulder peered into her sex; a shimmering hive. He was going to break her fragile heart. Since returning from the Costa Del Sol in November—a trip he spent perspiring and reading, in and out of feverish consciousness in a stinking hostel crawling with insects—he'd aligned himself with a duo of coworkers (Dane Bell—fiction editor, a Dutch-speaking Geordie with an NUFC tattoo on his lower neck, a pack-a-day Marlboro addiction and a taste for guttural literature, which is to say he was heavily involved in the scouting and publishing of writers reading deep, no-holds-barred prose in the underground pits and open mics of Groningen's most graffitied sectors—and Joan Laisne, an American expat who studied literature at Groningen University and simply never left the city, the fastest and most accurate proofreader on staff, who'd spent the past nine years telling herself the next manuscript she reviewed would be her last) who conspired to oust Daalmans for her mismanagement of the Borschau name—a responsibility she inherited from her father, Coen Daalmans, who died of liver failure in spring '97, and who founded the press with a mission to publish challenging works whose artistic idiosyncrasies built loyal readership and garnered positive regional attention without selling out to the contemporary consumerist ramp-up culture of sensationalistic masturbatory bestseller pulp. Point of order, with regard to Mila Daalmans' lean toward mass-market philistinism, the August publication of *Autosarcophagy* constituted a last straw, or the straw that broke the camel's back, or a short straw for the role of radicalizing agent due to its poor sentence structure and lack of discernible intent beyond the presentation of gore for gore's sake. At pub tables with overflowing ashtrays and tall glasses of draught lager, the three coworkers mocked and celebrated the book's critical failure, and joked that Daalmans might oust herself with a few more greenlights of similar quality. All the same, they made plans to demonstrate their dissent, and the flushing began in early December, only weeks before the millennium party that would launch him, in the space of one clandestine custodial orgasm, into the arms of a contradictory allegiance—a double life both for and against her. Under the desk two months later, Mulder coiled into himself, into the kaleidoscope of his mind where Mila Daalmans took the form of a sash or silk kerchief caught on a branch in a sturdy breeze, and he tasted the phantom salt of her neck and felt her fingernails teasing his scrotum and realized with a fatal pang that he might be falling in love with her.

***

At 3:07 pm on Thursday, April 13th, 2000, graphic novelist Rita Hoek stood at her whiteboard, which occupied an entire wall of her 40-square-meter studio apartment, storyboarding a chapter of the work she believed would become her breakthrough. The window was open, and over the blare of her plastic boombox, which played a cassette of Neil Young's *Harvest,* trains rumbled and bicycles ticked along Lodewijkstraat, and the spring breeze through flowering trees sent breaths of perfumed air to her nose. Hoek's breakthrough work, although officially untitled, was dubbed *Smoke* when she jotted notes about it in her journal, or drew character sketches during breaks at the movie theater where she worked, or simply when she envisioned the piece stretched out in her mind; a vibrant, savage tapestry; a post-postmodern meta-Bayeux. (Especially given its unfinished state and its projected magnanimity, the comparison to this historical artifact made sense in her mind.) *Smoke* was a throwback to 2nd-wave feminism, set in a steampunk, anarcho-dystopian future in which women walked around with the dicks of slain patriarchs hanging from their belts. Ironically, as severed dicks became memetically entrenched as status symbols, dick-measuring contests became commonplace. In the chapter Hoek was storyboarding at 3:07 pm on Thursday, April 13, 2000, one such contest was under way, and as she sketched the torches that lit the scene, so immersed was Hoek in her world she could actually smell, intermingled with the scent of spring blossoms, undercurrents of burning petrol.

***

In the diamond room at Groningen's Buurtcentrum Centraal the Progress Keepers gathered on metal folding chairs left behind by the 6 pm meeting of Narcotics Anonymous, which also yielded a half-plate of *kletskoppen* and a lingering smell of cigarette smoke. As the clock ticked round to quarter-past seven, Moeder Baas took the podium in her mask, cassock and characteristic black lipstick, and opened the meeting with an invocation of Pannekoek's "Darwinism and Marxism" before proceeding to general announcements: First, she said, it is Broer De Jong's birthday on December 18th so everyone is invited to his house this Saturday, 2 o'clock. *Gefeliciteerd*, Broer De Jong. Second, a reminder to clean up after yourselves at the end of each meeting—the knitting club has complained again. Last, with the tragic passing of Zus Bakker last weekend, we are in need of a new treasurer. Please see me after the meeting if you are interested, *is goed?* An impatient murmur rose from the congregation. They were all dressed in tunics and masks, and the heater was cranked to 30°C. Beads of sweat formed on foreheads. Moisture pooled inside armpits, knee pits, crotches, butt cracks. Excepting Broer de Jong, who appreciated the *gezelligheid* of his birthday recognition, nobody cared about the announcements—they were there a month before the *openbaring* to hear about one thing and one thing only: Moeder Baas' take on the half-eaten hand.

***

After another frustrating day at Brooklyn's 90th precinct, through which he garnered little information regarding his daughter's murder (which the cops maintained was suicide), Jinhai Tsang stood awaiting the L train back to The City. Although sparsely populated, the subway station at Montrose and Bushwick felt like a physical manifestation of hell, the beating heart of a fever-dream, or the cavernous ovens beneath a south-border death camp. He swung his satchel around to his front, unzipped its outer pocket, and pressed his back to the cool steel of the platform support. The book was tattered, spoked with little numbered tabs demarcating points of interest, left behind by officer Morales, the detective assigned to Helen's case who concluded for Jin that the book, the notes, the whole damn thing was meaningless— she had failed to parse causation from his daughter's annotations. And perhaps it was simply the sweat in his eyes or the fury-hangover from a day spent navigating red tape, but Jin experienced the same failure now as he skimmed the margins: Helen's notes seemed foreign, nonsensical, penned in languages long extinct. For the first time ever, he found himself wondering who his daughter had become. Along the platform, a bucket drummer drummed with the rapidity of machine-gun fire, and their composition or improvisation—their cacophony, Jin thought—echoed along the grimy tile, past where he stood perusing the book, into the darkness of the subway tunnel, its cumulative density broken only by the wind that preceded the train. At his desk that night, he spread the book open like a pinned specimen and began taking notes of his own. Across the loft, his wife, Lin Tsang, watched the news with tears in her eyes. There were stories of wildfires and tropical storms and floods and droughts and summer hail and headlines about stocks and fossil fuels and images of foreign wars and alt-right extremists chanting with signs, there were segments regarding digital privacy, profiles of women who were raped in the metaverse, a statistical roundup of ecological collapse, the most alarming of which was that 6.8% of all frog species were now extinct, a marked acceleration against estimates that 10% of all frogs would disappear by 2100. In that moment, time's linearity was as incontrovertible to Lin as the existence of spores in the building's walls, the screech of traffic on the streets outside, the immutability of Earth's rotation as it hung in orbit around the sun. She bowed her head and thought about Helen, the space dust inside her—inside them all— and the slow filtration of humanity's light across the infinite universe. What planet, a billion light years away, might witness their past from its far-off future, powerless to change anything?

***

In the library stood bookshelves built from oak trees fifty, one hundred, three hundred years old, hacked and felled and stripped and hewn and squared and sawn and lathed and screwed and sanded and varnished and lacquered and dried until they were unrecognizable as organisms, and onto their corpses were placed other trees, trees that arguably met worse ends, pulped and processed into translucent leaves, pressed and treated and stamped and sewn side by side in sarcophagal fans that humans called books—books belonging to Basil Small, who did not read as avidly as his collection suggested, but remained content to sit in proximity to the massacred trees, scouring the internet for photos of himself with various celebrity guests on *Codswallop!*, the perennially popular panel quiz show broadcast on Channel 4 from 1983 to 2035 with Small hosting from 1986 until 2017, when he was replaced by somebody younger and livelier, with straighter, whiter teeth and thicker, darker hair. *Codswallop!* was essentially a TV version of the board game Balderdash, in which contestants were asked to identify the correct definitions of nonsensical-sounding words, often with hilarious results. As Rachael Watson ran her finger over the book spines, the tick of her fingernails brought to mind Basil's show-laugh; loud and robotic, nothing like his actual laugh, which was silent and nasal and rather resembled suffocation, although to see joy come into his eyes was a joy unto itself, and life without joy was like life without trees; asphyxial. Each spine her finger brushed held a unique tactility, whether ragged leather or smooth pulp stock, but beneath the spines they all felt the same; a phalanx of collated pages. So when she came to a book whose innards felt squishy—or at least comparatively pliable—she stopped short and looked at the spine. The book was on a shelf set far from the window, in the dark recesses of the southeast corner where, if a trick door or other hidden egress were to exist, it would not come as a heart-stopping surprise. The surprise came when Watson opened the book to find its pages hollowed. In the scooped-out rectangle was a clear plastic bag. Her arm jerked. The bag containing the mummified hand was momentarily airborne before falling to the hardwood like a feather in a net.

***

At age 6, Aaliyah Foals was brought before a man in a white lab coat who shined a strobe light into her eyes and asked her to describe what she saw. The light on her face was silent and blue. As she stared into its core, the world in her peripheral vision gained speed and smeared into a nauseous blur, until all that remained was the light and the splotches it left on her mind; a twinkling array of concentric circles, braided filaments, a quincunx of stars set bright on a background of muted pink. She returned to the room lying flat on her back, the man in the lab coat crouched above her. His cheeks were pocked with tiny scars; a face of lunar topography. Tell me, he said. What did you see?

***

Following the 48th iteration of the *Robbens* AI news anchor program, the three human engineers responsible for its maintenance were made redundant, and the Eindhoven-based corporation to which its patents belonged—Intejer Platformix; Euronext ticker INTPLAT—suspended production at the behest of its legal department, following the discovery that *48-Robbens* had caused the company to commit libel against itself. The retrospective, which was made public as part of IntPlat's 2037 shareholder update, claims the libelous output resulted from negative feedback loops in the AI's algorithm. News segments published automatically to the Global-Metaneural-News-Network (following script edits by the *Levin* AI copyeditor program, which was still operational) became progressively untrustworthy as *Robbens'* machine-learning capabilities matured. Although the outgoing tech team identified the cause of these feedback loops, its members noted that rolling back would undermine the software's objective function. Through a series of escalating advancements, the AI concluded that realistic lies were more profitable than facts with regard to the currency of metaverse engagement, which was quantified in each GMNN segment's monetizable metadata, including biometric responses such as pupil dilation and resting pulse variance, and constituted 100% of the program's RTD. The retrospective states that in reaction to this discovery, *Robbens* began to eschew its own vetoers, amending its output to maximize impressions despite legal exposure. Indeed, even the auto-libelous content showed a return some 20% higher than the typical take. The tech team's recommendation was to modify the algorithm's objective function to weight profitability below credibility, and add penalties to exclude IntPlat from its output. The executive recommendation was to sell the AI as an out-of-box solution to businesses in the clickbait industry, whose business models had baked-in libel funds. The board approved of the latter, and contracts were drafted that insulated IntPlat from all liability related to *Robbens'* usage. In the decades to come, *48-Robbens* carried out its objective function unabated, and the shareholders for whom it generated capital grew old and weak, and died like every human before them.

***

From the shadows, they peered across the undulating glow the string lanterns cast on the bar patio where their three colleagues—Bell, Laisne, and Mulder—sat in treasonous languor, steeped in their sedition while cigarette smoke rose blue to the light's terminus and disappeared like ink into an inverted inkwell. I've got you now, they said to the air. Just you *verraders* wait and see.

***

The idea to ally with the Progress Keepers came organically, as Dane Bell had already procured information about their cause via a birthday party on December 18th, a full three months before the flushing game surfaced and Daalmans went on her firing spree. He attended the party at his cousin's behest, as she was an acquaintance of the celebrant—a kid named de Jong with a voice like a carbon monoxide detector. Bell expected to mingle and chat and drink a few pints, keep his cousin company before departing to the pub to watch The Toon wallop Bradford. What he discovered, having never attended a traditional Dutch birthday party, was that alcohol and mingling were not on the agenda. Every random chair in the gaff was placed in a circle in a cramped living room that smelled of mildew and cinnamon, and after congratulating each other incessantly, everyone sat in that big random circle and downed tea and cake for five hours straight. During this time, nobody switched places—to do so was considered poor taste. Whoever you were stuck with was who you were stuck with. To his dismay, Bell was seated at the opposite end of the circle to his cousin, and was saddled instead with a fat bloke named Boer, who saw Bell was black and heard his accent and decided that was reason enough when coupled with his name to tell a joke about the Boer War. His laugh was like the buzz of a dying wasp. Finding no levity in Bell's expression, Boer turned to converse with the octogenarian on his left. To Bell's right was a woman named Baas who smelled like the wind that blew off the North Sea. She was ugly and white and she wore black lipstick. After some slurping and bites of cake, she asked Bell what he thought of the news. Depends on the news, Bell said. And so they talked about the hand. She was ecstatic to find he knew all about it, and was especially enthralled that he brought her within two degrees of separation of its discoverer, Sylvio Gomes, who worked on Bell's floor and technically didn't discover a thing, but did own the dog to whom credit was due. Sylvio's a twat, Bell remarked. Baas sat back and sipped her tea. So what's your take? she said. My take? Bell said. Baas nodded. What do you think the hand symbolizes? Bell looked around for alcohol, clutched the pocket where he kept his fags. He glanced at Boer, the racist, who was talking contentedly with the elderly woman two chairs down, a woman who seemed to find Boer charming. Lighting a cigarette, and thinking it best not to pigeonhole himself with on-the-fly analysis of a mystery that held no greater meaning, Bell shrugged and blew smoke. Go ahead, then, what's yours?

***

On December 14th, 1999, 41-year-old Subinspector Juan Vela Sánchez of the Policía Local de Medina del Campo was leaning on the station reception desk, eating an apple and flirting with the receptionist—23-year-old Ana Sofia Herrera Romero—in hopes of taking her out for New Year's when the station doors opened to admit a man so filthy and sunburnt it appeared he'd been roasted over a bed of coals. Vela Sánchez paused mid-bite. The cooked man, whom the subinspector now realized was a delivery driver, was emaciated, shivering. His sleeves were stuffed into the kangaroo pocket of his Nacex jumpsuit, which was ripped and baggy, doused in green mud that stank like the canal, partially obscuring the company logo sewn across the torso. Outside, a gray wind pummeled the street. It could not be more than 10°C. No sign of a delivery van. The thought occurred to Subinspector Vela Sánchez: this man may actually have been intercepted en route and kidnapped before being cooked, boiled, chemically scalded or otherwise deliberately burnt. The office of the Directorate-General in Madrid had sent memos across the northern provinces warning of regional ETA flare-ups surrounding the trials of Enrique Rodríguez Galindo and Julen Elgorriaga, the Spanish officials charged with complicity in the kidnapping, torture and execution of two ETA members—Lasa and Zabala—while commanding one of the Ministerio del Interior's secretive GAL death squads in 1983. *¿Qué pasó, señor?* asked Ana Sofia Herrera Romero. The cooked man shivered more violently. In a voice full of splintered glass, he said he'd woken in a field west of town with no recollection of how he got there, no recollection of where he'd been, no recollection of who he was. The subinspector clapped his hands at the *policías* dozing in the bullpen, demanded a blanket and a working wheelchair, and two liters of mineral water. *¿Puede decirme su nombre, señor?* he said, turning back. But the cooked man was having a seizure. Limbs rigid, eyes rolled back, the man twitched on the floor like Saul of Tarsus on the road to Damascus. Vela Sánchez sprang forward and freed the man's arms from the kangaroo pocket, which acted as a straitjacket. *Santa mierda*, the subinspector whispered. The left hand was lost. All that remained was a gruesome stump; shoddily cauterized, oozing pus. Under the skin of the remaining forearm, the veins appeared to teem with black ink. *Llama a la ambulancia!* the subinspector ordered, and Ana Sofia Herrera Romero dialed 112. When the seizure passed and they had the cooked man safe in a wheelchair, the subinspector asked him what happened to the hand. *No sé*, the cooked man muttered. *No sé. No sé. No sé quién soy, inspector.* Then another seizure gripped him.

***

Corralling her two-year-old daughter with one arm and cradling her infant son in the other, Catalina Montero Respaldo held the telephone with her shoulder as she processed the news that their father had been found. Four months, *dios*. Where had he been? The voice on the other end was deadpan. It told her the details were fuzzy at best, and the non-deceased, afflicted with amnesia and acute epilepsy (to say nothing of his missing hand, or the skin-grafts he would undergo) was in no state to clarify. All the same, the voice said, your husband is alive, and that is an incredible thing. *Un milagro*, agreed Montero Respaldo. But Raúl Sanz Basurto is no longer my husband.

***

At 3:07 pm on Thursday, April 13th, 2000, parish priest William Sule was riding his bike along Lodewijkstraat, stewing on a violent (by clerical standards) altercation involving himself, his curate, and two triclavian ministers from St. Hermias Cathedral in Paddepoel, which began as a friendly debate, over tea, about the number of nails used in the crucifixion, and culminated in one of the ministers thrusting a liturgical candle in Pastor Sule's face, screaming in a belligerent Latin-Dutch hybrid while communion wine splattered the sacristy walls. Crossing the canal to run parallel the offices in Europapark, Pastor Sule could still feel the heat from the candle's flame and the thud of his heart in the holds of his torso, a whispered invocation of Christ, who partook of a feast of his own body and blood in the Cenacle at Jerusalem, gifting his grace to the famished world. Suddenly the handlebars jerked. A serpentine hiss emanated from the tires. As he yanked the brakes and skidded to a halt, the pastor craned his neck to the right to find the passage of time halting, too: Here at 3:07 pm on Thursday, April 13th, 2000, as though the machinations of his mind were manifest through a projective lens, the candle fire was physical, the flames licking like menacing tongues from the mouth of an inferno that spat heat toward him.

***

At age 15, brimming with inspiration from a community center poetry reading she attended that summer—or rather, a reading her foster guardians allowed her to attend—Aaliyah Foals began writing poems in a pocket-sized notebook she kept tucked into the kangaroo pocket of her overalls. The poems were short and not very good, but they were embers of her soul, and for that fact she cherished them. Her condition had stabilized insofar as it hadn't progressed beyond its original triggers (lights, tight spaces), but its non-degenerative nature made it no less debilitating. At night she lay up in her lumpy top bunk, afraid of the lasers under her eyelids, tweaking her poems by the streetlight that sliced through the gaps in the blinds. And during the day there was school. The rushing hormones, the effortless cruelty of impressionable children, the sanctuary of English class, the flickering strip lights of the school gymnasium, the brain-purling claustrophobia of mathematics, the bursting color of chemistry experiments, and throughout it all, the oppressive heat of eyes on her body—teachers, paraeducators, hall monitors, classmates—always present, glowing from some corner of her periphery, evincing expectations of imminent collapse. Surviving each afternoon, Aaliyah's walk home took her past a café called Brokehouse where she paused in awe at the haggard writers hunched over bloodstained manuscripts, the brothers engaged in political debates, the Sub Pop holdouts sipping coffee and smoking cigarettes. It was here at Brokehouse, on the crowded community bulletin board that she found the flier for her first contest: The

Arthur J. Murphy Poetry Prize, hosted by local lit mag *Chum*, which Aaliyah hadn't read before, hadn't seen on newsstands before, but which had the resources to print a poster and pay out a winner. The top prize was publication, a *Chum* bumper sticker, and $150 cash. She entered by mail the next afternoon; a poem entitled *What Did You See?* and the five-dollar entry fee, which she sent in change from her piggy bank. Judgment was swift. Although no feedback accompanied the rejection, the editors enclosed the latest issue of *Chum*, insinuating that the key to better writing was packaged inside its glossy covers. The issue was 40 pages long and contained five individual contributions: A haiku series about slave labor and Starbucks; a short story set on Bainbridge Island; an essay about a Dutch Y2K cult, an office park fire and a severed hand (her favorite of the bunch, written by a local named Joan Laisne); a series of photos of crustpunk kids living on sidewalks in Portland, Oregon; and a prose-poem about Al Gore's nose. Night in her bunk, orange streetlight slicing in, Aaliyah read the issue cover to cover, over and over, obsessively devouring *Chum* until her eyelids grew too heavy to hold. And by day, she went about her adolescence with the words of those pieces unleashed inside her; stoking her embers, filling her notebook with prosperous ash. A month later, the towers fell. One night in early November, the streetlight outside her window went out; a shorted lightbulb. The city never repaired it.

***

Like school-age truants brought before the headmistress, they stood three abreast in Daalmans' office with the stink of her serenity candles and her question lingering in the air around them. *Why did they do it?* The candles flickered. Mulder coughed. Bell embodied a coiled spring. As Joan Laisne stood in spiteful silence, she felt a great urge to sew her nose shut. Daalamans, visibly perturbed or else running some elaborate computation, rubbed her temples and tried again. *Ik ben niet achterlijk*, she said. And maybe I don't need to hear you say it. I know this whole thing is a dig at me, and that's fine; ever since I took the reins I've received nothing but side-eyes and attitude. But I don't understand why you'd take it out on the toilets. The damage to the ladies' room alone is...well. And then this book. She leaned forward onto her elbows. At least tell me what's wrong with this book? Sylvio's notes called it transgressive, edgy...Borschau through and through. Again, her words ran into silence. Laisne looked down the line at her accomplices. Dane was focused on a point in the air ten centimeters in front of his nose. Mulder was glazed, seemingly absent, eyes pointed toward his shoes. It seemed he was processing something unique; his features assumed an alien quality, a skin-deep compartmentalism, as though his eyes and nostrils and philtrum and lips were all somehow borrowed from separate faces. Finally, worn down beneath the heat of the candles and the nervous, awkward vibe in the room, Joan surrendered to her tongue: Have you actually read this book? she said. Daalmans' feet began to tap. 'Borschau through and through,' Laisne mocked. We're an arthouse publisher, Mila. This book isn't *art*. It's what's left of art after the business end eats its soul. It's insipid, shock-value, for-profit bullshit like 90% of the stuff your new hires submit. And don't get me started on *Sylvio*. The guy doesn't know literature from latrinalia, and we're meant to feel bad for flushing his project? We did the press a fucking favor. Joan took a shaky breath. She was floating above herself like a storm. The men were quiet. The flames danced. The smell was atrocious. Daalmans stared at Laisne—through her—expression caught in a disappointed tangle. At last she said in a fragile voice, Does everybody feel this way? Dane Bell fingered his ear. Aye, he said. I'm with Joanie. Mulder remained transfixed by his loafers. Sorry, Mila, he murmured. Through the window, the sky curled like a dying leaf. Spits of rain etched the glass. Squinting out, Laisne was certain—at long last, relieved— that the manuscript she was currently proofreading was destined to be her last.

***

Two months into his first major relapse since returning from a stint at the surf-therapy detox in Monte Redondo, Anthony Small was sitting in his luxury Knightsbridge apartment, snorting cheap cocaine cut with loperamide and watching a DJ Skoptics livestream when a restricted number called his phone. A voice came through, tinny and distant. Small leaned forward to turn down the music. The voice spoke of a call Anthony had placed two years prior; an inquiry at the behest of a client who sought a talisman of continued prosperity. The artifact had been inaccessible at the time, but was now, miraculously, almost desperately, available for purchase. Small racked his brain, inhaled a bump off the end of his house key. He must have been higher than he thought. Come again? he said. *The hand*, the voice whispered. I have gone to great lengths. Small laughed so hard he almost fell off the couch. Mate, he said, you didn't? No jokes right, I forgot all about it. The voice was silent. Hello? Small said. Hello, the voice replied. It was a strange voice. European. Impatient. Small had heard this voice before. He imagined the lips that curled around it; chapped and angry in the spotlight of his mind. Two more lips materialized as well, slightly too smooth and full for their age. When *Channel 4* replaced him as *Codswallop!* host in 2018, Anthony's father, Basil, endured an unprecedented period of paranoia and desperation, fueled, Anthony assumed, by fear of obscurity, non-entity, lost celebrity—that is, *poverty*—and this culminated in a strange request. Four years prior to being sacked, Basil had eaten dinner with a female guest-star who spoke of a severed hand in Holland—a hand, supposedly, with magical properties; the ability to safeguard status—to secure completely the social, financial, and political interests of anyone bold enough to possess it. The story was codswallop. Why Basil tasked Anthony with the hand's procurement was never made clear, but regardless, Anthony assumed his father, aware of his son's history regarding the portation of certain goods, made a judgment call to keep this bizarre request in the family for fear that the paparazzi might crucify him. Stone sober at the time, and never expecting the hand to exist, much less become available for purchase, Anthony told his dad no promises, placed a few calls to the Netherlands, and went on snorting his life into silver before overdosing and attending the surf-therapy program in Monte Redondo. Two years later, with his face, nose, and throat turning numb, Anthony breathed into his cellphone and weighed the odds that the call was a prank. Please, he thought, let this be real. He'd pulled a memory out of the fog; a memory that made his heart doubletime (or maybe his addiction just took the wheel): A hushed exchange through a cracked car window, a strange solemnity to his father's voice: Whatever it takes, Anthony, I don't care to haggle. When it's in my hands, you can name your price.

***

Clinical records following Anneke "Moeder" Baas' April 13th, 2000, arrest state she was detained on charges of conspiracy to commit arson, disturbing the peace, and criminal trespassing. They also indicate that at the time, she did not hold claim to a lease or deed within Groningen city limits, nor Holland, Europe, Asia, Africa, Oceania, or the Americas. She received mail at a maisonette on Willemstraat, the owner of which—a Mr. Hamid Bensaïd—had outstanding petitions to mandate her eviction. During her intake interview at the Groningen-Noord Forensic Psychiatric Center, the following descriptors were applied to her demeanor: Combative, impatient, paranoid, dissociative. When asked to elucidate her motives for the ritualistic biblioclasm to which she was party, she spat in the attending clinician's face and attempted to free herself from her restraints. For everyone's safety, staff anaesthetist Cristi Vlasenko administered 2.5mg of haloperidol into the patient's left thigh. In notes attached to his initial diagnosis, Dr. Wilfried Bernd, who spent two years at the Universität der Künste Berlin before switching his focus to clinical psychology, wrote that Baas' actions were, in his opinion, manifestations of paranoia exacerbated by the pressures of imminent homelessness, self-indoctrination, and narcissism. This is a woman,

Bernd wrote, who until the sun rose on January 1st, 2000, believed the world as she knew it was destined to end on New Year's Day. She refers to Y2K as the *openbaring*—an as-yet unrealized societal cleansing that was supposed to usher forth from the turning of the millennium. Having stepped outside on New Year's morning to find the city still gripped by what she refers to as "*De Rechterhand*," however, Ms. Baas experienced a personal aberration more powerful than any millenarian event. It is my clinical opinion, Bernd continued, that Anneke's need to rationalize the unchanged continuation of our society has forced her to assume a sense of stewardship over the *openbaring*—a responsibility whose weight has both agitated her dissociative tendencies and radicalized her physical influence over the misguided members of her sect, whose blind obedience, despite her self-image first and foremost as a servant, triggers her NPD. More analysis is required to pinpoint root causes. Recommend immediate administration to inpatient care and clozapine titration to determine dosage. The doctor took notes in a spiral notebook with blue-ruled paper and 1-inch margins down the left-hand side. In one such margin, a doodle appears, followed by a larger version among the back pages:

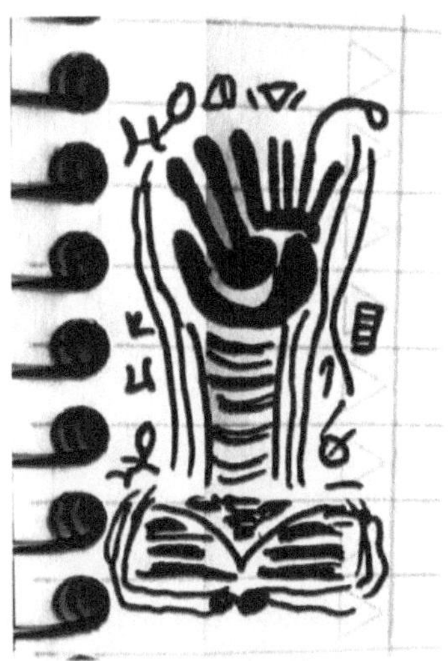

EA31-A; C.B. Bernd, W.
Case no. 124294-B;
C/O PB Groningen, 2000

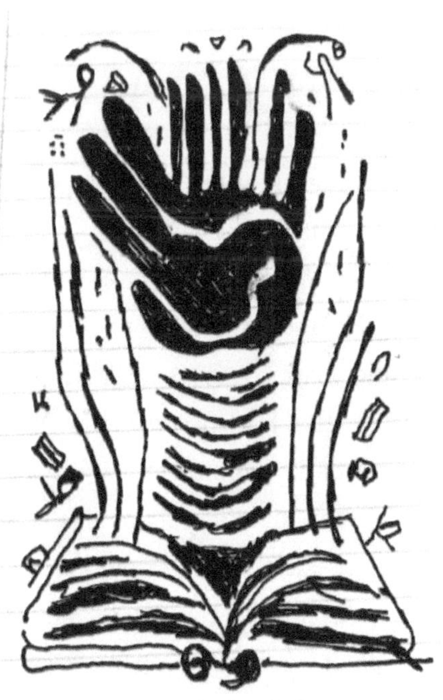

EA31-B; C.B. Bernd, W.
Case no. 124294-B;
C/O PB Groningen, 2000

Years later, responding to a call from a concerned neighbor, police found Dr. Bernd in his flat, slumped and bloated at the kitchen table with an empty bottle of Nembutal in his lap and dozens of hand-drawn versions of this image hanging around him on white-wire clotheslines.

***

A month into her sophomore year studying literature at University of Washington (an institution that put her deeply in debt), Aaliyah Foals had a seizure at a Halloween party that changed the trajectory of her life forever. As she ran outside with tears in her eyes and broke through the crowd of smokers on the porch, she felt eyes on her body, her skin and her hair; eyes with the heat of dance-floor lights and the metallic 9-volt buzz of the air as her consciousness swept away from her. As she started down the block alone, she heard laughter, jeering, the lilting prattle of drunk male voices, insinuations and innuendoes, privilege and pride and imminent puke. Back home she lay on her bed and gripped the sheets as the room spun around her. She stared at the cracks in the ceiling paint and whispered gently, willing the cracks to open their mouths and swallow her into their plaster guts. In that moment, for the first time ever, she found herself desperate to traverse her own brain; to map its passageways, paint its corruption on translucent slides and watch the neurons light up her skull like fireworks bursting against overcast sky. The following week she declared a new major, and four years later, the semester following her 23rd birthday, she completed the requirements for her neuroscience degree and set about applying to graduate programs.

***

It wasn't until the fumes reached his nose that Christiaan Mulder, former Borschau fiction editor and chronic cougher reborn into an acute and glossy delirium on a trip to Spain he couldn't explain, realized he was in too deep. They had gathered after lunch as planned. Per the arrangement, hatched in the diamond room two weeks prior, all 26 members of the Progress Keepers, now including Mulder, Laisne and Bell, had acquired many copies of the infamous book (leftover from the boxes swiped in preparation for flushing) and arrived ready to usher forth the *openbaring*. After a brief spell huddled beneath the *Linkerhand* banner, waiting for the rain to subside, Moeder Baas stood with her back to the building, which caught the afternoon sun in its panes, and gave her address. The usual themes. *Rechterhand* and *verantwoordelijkheid* and *het verdriet van de onderdrukten*. Time accelerated. The books were placed in a tinderous pile. From a Renault Clio parked nearby, a plastic petrol can was produced. The accelerant was poured. The fumes rose thick and dizzying. Mulder's heart galloped. Today, said Baas, we set fire to the veins of the old world order that the blaze may rush to every extremity, and from the ashes...She struck a match, but before she could speak it sizzled out. She tutted and repeated, From the ashes...Another match. Another hiss. Baas' face contorted with fury, or what appeared as fury in her lower features, visible below her eye mask as she fumbled with the little matchbox. *From* the ashes, she said more forcefully, we shall be *reborn*. This time the match stayed lit, and as it hit the doused pyre the flames kicked to life with a percussive whoosh, the pages caught and curled and blackened and ashes rose in snowlike drifts and Mulder—Christiaan Mulder, born in Utrecht to a mother battling methaqualone addiction, a father battling existentialist malaise with malbec, an uncle with sharp hands and pallid skin—felt the unbattened hatches of his soul flung wide. He ran until he was clear of the smoke, rasping along the *Oude Winschoterdiep* where he tore off his eye mask and slipped the tunic over his head and threw both clumsily into the canal before sprinting on, shirtless and scratching, asking *when* and *how* and *where*, until in the moody blackness of the crisp pre-dawn he arrived at Groningen Airport Eelde, where he bought a ticket and boarded an airplane bound for somewhere else in the world.

***

Having arrived for work the night of April 13th to discover the building's exterior walls, windows, and entryways caked with coagulated ash and tar, Peter Garminski poked a discerning eye down the barrel of his life and decided it was time to pull the trigger. A week later, being nocturnal with nothing to occupy his nights, Garminski got drunk, wandered into a boxing gym in Kostverloren, and told the trainer he wanted to fight professionally. The trainer, a German named Hogrefe with a crooked nose, looked Garminski up and down—his puffy face, his ropy arms, his beer gut and columnal legs with bones misshapen by years of pushing broom and crouching in strange positions to wipe up grime—and said he'd train him if he came back sober, even let him spar a little, but a ring-fighter he was not and never would be. To pretend otherwise would be irresponsible. Incensed, offended, outraged, defeated, Garminski backpedaled through the exit and slammed the door behind him. In the fresh night air he followed the Eendrachtskanaal southeast toward the museum bridge where he picked a fight with a PCP addict called Thunderchicken, who punched him so hard his eye socket collapsed and nasal bone fragments traveled into his sinus, causing blood to pool in his airways as he lay unconscious in the gray streetlight.

***

After 52 consecutive years on air, the decision to shut down *Codswallop!* production was executed following a season of abysmal ratings that began with the replacement of the show's third host, Raj Varma (who replaced Basil Small in 2017), as part of a profitability crunch that saw Varma replaced with an AI host called *12-Trebek*, contracted from the Eindhoven-based tech corporation Intejer Platformix. Generating for *BizBuzz* in 2035, *47-Robbens* called the overhaul ill-conceived, noting that the decision to automate toward cost savings, ironically, brought about the cannibalization-death of a tenured revenue stream and likely put the studio deeper in the red. Writing for *Telly* later that year, TV critic Noel Dickinson mourned the show's end, but stated it was not a surprise: Not only did the switch to a robotic host mark a downturn in general production value, Dickinson wrote, it also denoted a creepy evolution in the studio's economic strategy. Frankly, he wrote, it was just plain creepy. The AI host, whose namesake is no doubt turning in his grave, was stuck so deep in the uncanny valley that even the celebrity guests—who thereafter abandoned the programme for good—lost all semblance of humanity themselves. The piece wore on in an equally judgmental fashion, and ended with the following kicker: May this historic loss act as a lesson. There are some jobs robots cannot do. That, my friends, is no codswallop.

***

Writing for *Dagblad Martinistad* in August 2000, arts reporter Nathalie Ryskamp called the book a cancer: That this vomitrocious anthology was published in the first place, she wrote, is an issue. That its hold over some readers is powerful enough to inspire acts of religious zealotry, acts of arson, even acts mirroring its abominable content, is nothing short of a societal blight. 1 out of 5 stars, only because zero is not an option.

***

Following their release and subsequent depositions, conducted by the lawyers at De Brauw Blackstone Westbroek N.V. on behalf of the building's owner, Yufei Li, who aimed to expel Borschau from his property and obtain remuneration for the extensive fire, ash and smoke damage the incident caused, as well as for the assuagement of the Garminski siblings, who blamed the death of their brother—a recovering alcoholic in need of stability—on the hazardous working conditions that inspired Peter to quit (conditions, the complaint alleged, that Li allowed his tenant to foment), Dane Bell and Joan Laisne found themselves standing in the car park, staring at the stain where the books had been burned. Ground zero, Laisne said. Aye, said Bell. Have you heard from Mulder? Laisne asked. Bell lit a cigarette. Slippery cunt left toon ah reckon. Then they hugged and said good luck, and went their separate ways in life. Though many specifics remain private, the following have been confirmed: Dane Bell returned to Newcastle and curated a chapbook anthology series called *Contagion*, which sold in underground literary circles, at readings and house shows and generally anywhere else he could flog them. According to a 2008 blurb in *The Sunday Sun*, Bell was once stabbed in a pub in Gateshead, whereupon he finished his pint and paid his tab before walking outside and hailing a taxi to drive him to A&E. His social media, metaverse and physical footprints are shallow, if not entirely dormant. His whereabouts today are unknown. Joan Laisne flew to Cyprus, Egypt, Morocco, Majorca, and lastly to Portugal before an urgent call that her father was sick drew her back to the States, specifically to Puyallup, WA, where she was born. Here, with the words of a thousand Borschau manuscripts swirling like stars in the grief-stricken galaxies of her mind she began writing essays, short stories and poems about her time in Holland, many of which appeared in print and online publications founded or specializing in artists from the PNW, including *Eggbag Review, Titlark Editions, Flograg Review, Literace, Chum, Lighthouse Literary Review* and others. A steady stream of published credits carried her name between 2001 and 2016, when abruptly her output ceased. Her Twitter went dark. She deleted Facebook (as so many did). Following this, her most public appearance came on a billboard for the Tacoma Museum of Glass, which stood on the side of Interstate-5 for eighteen months between 2026 and 2028. On the billboard, Laisne could be seen with her elderly mother, walking the background of a colorful photo designed to attract drive-by tourists passing through town on their way north from Portland. Laisne's whereabouts are unknown, but presumably she is still alive, residing somewhere that both feeds and satisfies her wanderlust.

****

After the depositions were over and the court upheld Mr. Li's proposal to forcefully nullify the lease, and after her negligence as a tenant was entered into the record for future generations of archaeologists and legal scholars, and eco-resilient earth-inheritors to read, Mila Daalmans stood in the half-vacated Borschau office with a box in her arms, tensing her face to keep tears at bay. Around her, the remaining staff looked grim as they cleared their desks, muttering amongst themselves, shuffling across the red-penned papers that littered the carpets like marble slabs. Because it was once a palace. With a knot in her throat, she began emptying the room-length bookshelves that lined the far wall—the shelves where one copy of each new Borschau release was placed in celebration beside its predecessors. These shelves were at capacity long before she inherited the press. With each new release, the leftmost book on the topmost shelf was removed and the remaining books on the topmost shelf were shifted left so the leftmost book on the second shelf down could relocate to the rightmost slot of the topmost shelf, leaving an open slot in its place. The second-shelf books were then shifted left, and so on down all five shelves until an empty slot appeared at the rightmost edge of the lowest shelf, and the newest title assumed its place at the head of the snake. The departing book was taken to a storage facility on Peizerweg, where a hard-copy archive of Borschau's entire catalog was kept in climate-controlled cryogenesis until such a time as its reanimation (or destruction) was necessary. As she worked her way along the spines, a lugubrious fog encumbered Mila's periphery; the same feeble yellowish fog that crowded the whites of her father's eyes before he slipped away for good. She thought about the fire and the rain outside, about ancient embers transported in hollow logs, the pull of regret on her faculties, the ball of her heel pulverizing sacred coals. She thought about the comforting blandness of home. She thought about Christiaan. Wondered where on earth he could be. She wondered where he stood within the sphere of his own physiology; which plane he'd visited inside himself that turned him into what he became. And she wondered whether the Mulder she knew was simply an amalgamation of complex expectations, first impressions and gray matter (a concept object, such as a clock, which has time applied to it), or something altogether worse; something enigmatic and bold, something deliberate in its propensity to hurt. And she wondered the same about her father. And she wondered the same about herself. As the last book dropped into the box bound for limbo on Peizerweg, Mila Daalmans went on wondering, and after that she wondered some more.

***

By age 36, Dr. Aaliyah Veronica Foals had contributed more to the field of neuroscience than anyone might reasonably expect given her circumstances. After graduating from UW in 2011, she earned her PhD at OHSU, where her research into seizure imaging at the Jungers Center earned her nominations for multiple awards—including an SFN Young Investigator Award— and set her career on a fruitful track. In the years that followed, working as an associate at The Allen Institute and still afflicted with the compulsion to write, she published groundbreaking articles on the subjects of epileptic liminality (with particular regard to *petit mal* absence seizures), seizure origination & hypersynchrony,

& hemiconvulsion-hemiplegia syndrome in children, among others. As a consultant to the team responsible for developing the first zebrafish model of epileptic cognitive dysfunction, she was invited to a dinner in Montreal, attended by some of the brightest minds in her field, new and old, at which she made conversation with Dr. Pilar Alvarez Santos, deputy director of the Cajal Institute in Madrid, who offered her a job she did not refuse, but which filled her with dread—a dread she did not understand nor seek to properly decode. When she left the States, she left nothing in particular behind. While she reveled in her profession, she spent every Christmas alone, owed interest over principal on multiple loans, was unsuccessful at dating, and went about her waking hours brimming with anxiety that everything she'd ever achieved was happening to someone else, a being whose dream she inhabited. Her own epilepsy was generalized, tonic, originating from both hemispheres, which left ablation and lobectomy off the table, and while she grasped firmly the specifics of its triggers, her condition remained as inescapable to her as the allure of scientific discovery. Spain was simply the next frontier. So in 2022, surrendered inexorably to her life's true calling, Dr. Foals found herself disembarking a train in Vallehermoso, bound for *Los Nogales Reina Victoria* assisted living facility, where she was to meet her newest subject. The attending nurse led her down the hall to the common area.

The blinds were open and dusty sunlight cast parallelograms on the carpet. There were armchairs and couches and a little TV, and shuffling around were patients with dementia and emphysema and other afflictions with their own distinct smells. The nurse paused in the double-doorway. *Aha—ahí está,* he said. In a chair near the window, a patient with long, oily black hair sat hunched over a bowl of green grapes. He was wearing aviator sunglasses, and as they approached, Foals realized he was missing one hand. *Raúl?* the nurse said. *Esta es la doctora Foals.* Raúl did not move. *Hola, Raúl,* Aaliyah said, as cordially as she could muster, although the sight of his stump plucked a dissonant chord. With the vacant composure of a three-toed sloth, Raúl turned his head to look. His neck tensed, his glasses vibrated, and as the seizure gripped him the bowl hit the carpet and grapes scattered all over the floor. Some nights later, lying in bed and pondering with intrigue Raúl's imaging—which revealed atypical impulses in the dorsolateral prefrontal right cortex every time he had a seizure—Aaliyah turned in her mind the possibility that a triggering event could manifest like a ghost in the abandoned neural passageways of a damaged brain. The organ was a beautiful enigma. Raúl Sanz Basurto was a beautiful shell; his trigger event was sad and compelling, his stumped left-wrist a strange souvenir. Her eyelids grew heavy. The sounds of Madrid grew distant and dull. And just as she was drifting off, prompted perhaps by the orange streetlight that sliced through the gaps in the bedroom shutters, something in her memory clicked, and she felt her own brain flicker to life. Two weeks later, having followed the breadcrumbs of the scientific method to the giddy suspense of a testable hypothesis, Foals placed a call that carried her voice northeast across Europe, into the ear of a Dutch operator who transferred her into the bowels of the earth to an evidence locker brimming with relics. The next morning she packed her bag, buttoned her cardinal red silk blouse and boarded a plane to the Netherlands, where an evidence clerk named Marilyn De Groot was expecting her.

***

In 2020, a fortnight before his retirement, Jaan Peltz was summoned to a Zoom call with the forensic lab supervisor's office in room 2A of the Politiebureau Groningen Centrum, and told he was losing his pension. Evidently, his leaking confidential information to the press—especially the leftist rag *Dagblad Martinistad*, which began using suspiciously detailed case specifics to run clickbait headlines about the bureau following the American ACAB upheaval that summer—was not only frowned upon, but a violation of his NDA, and technically cause for prosecution. The press, it seemed, had sprung a leak of its own. Given Peltz' proximity to retirement and the state of global employment under COVID-19, the bureau showed leniency with regard to his termination's immediacy. They gave Peltz two paid weeks to wrap up any remaining work before vacating his station, and offered him a modest severance. The revocation of his pension was non-negotiable. Two weeks later, enraged, brimming with fear at the prospect of old age and destitution (a lethal combination), Peltz made as his last act of duty a visit to the cold-case evidence locker in sub-basement 1F under the guise of referencing a fingerprint swatch. It was here beneath milky, tinkling striplights that Peltz thumbed through history to find his mark—case #124294-B—and exhumed his contingency plan.

****

At 1400 hours on Tuesday, July 21st, 2026, Detective Marquisa Morales of Brooklyn's 90th Precinct was called into her superiors' office to deliver an update on the Tsang investigation. Lieutenant Joe Magaddino and Sergeant Niecy Roebuck sat at their desks expectantly. What's the status, Detective? We're closing the case as a suicide, Morales said. There's no evidence of foul play here, despite the insistence of Tsang's father, who seems unwilling or unable to process the situation. Basically, she was just some depressive who found a way out. And what's your read on this book? Sgt. Roebuck said. Is it dangerous? Detective Morales glanced at the wall where there hung a photograph of the topmost NYPD hierarchy, about fifteen White men posing in dress blues. Well, Ma'am, as far as I can tell, it's just the notes of someone with a wild imagination. *Time as a circulatory system. Fate as the branches on a tree. Blood as the shoes on a horse. God as a self-consuming tongue. Death ventricle. Birth atrium...*It all *sounds* meaningful, but there's no mention of any of it in the book's actual text, and we can't find any other matches. Lt. Magaddino picked up a photocopy from the folder on his desk. And these codes inside the back cover, he said. 2038, TD22, 5340.32, RSB99...what do they mean? Detective Morales shrugged. We cross-referenced every number in there. Zero hits. No terrorist cells, organized crime or gang affiliations, IP addresses, dark web alphanumerics...nothing. If they had any meaning— and sorry if this sounds insensitive, Lieutenant—that meaning died with Helen Tsang. Our best guess at this point is something to do with cryptocurrency; a list of tickers or future tickers, or else something to do with the metaverse. She was left-leaning. Decentralize the internet, decentralize the economy, defund the police, seize the means of production, yada yada yada. She spent all her time online with this stuff. Browsing history was full of it. The Lieutenant and Sergeant looked at each other. Anything that would indicate she was dangerous, or anyone would have cause to kill her? Detective Morales shrugged. A few small arguments here and there. Some racial slurs came her way, someone blamed her for COVID-19. The Nazi word went out that way. Nothing worthy of murder. A Swatting maybe, but not murder. Like I said, she was just a depressed young woman with a hard-on for Marx. Lieutenant Magaddino closed his eyes in frustration. And the hand? The Dutch writing? The dates and charts? Morales shook her head. I'm sorry, Lieutenant. We just don't know.

***

Down the echoing subway-tiled hall from the armed entry doors, keys chimed as the bolt slid aside to admit Nurse Hendricks into the cage, where the overnight orderly Thomas Mertens sat watching the lounge through the meds window. It was 7:35 am and the patients had just come in from breakfast; sixteen in all, dressed in robes and scrubs and slippers; no jewelry, no belts, no shoelaces. Tough night? Hendricks asked as she opened the meds cupboard and began labeling paper cups. Mertens rubbed his bloodshot eyes. Halle woke up screaming and scratching again, he said. We gave her a shot of lorazepam. I'll push her Seroquel back to lunch, Hendricks said. Any others? The usual, Mertens said. Erin G got up at midnight and spun in circles next to the bed. Flora was awake at 4 am, masturbating and wailing. And then Anneke...well, look now, she's right on cue. Mertens nodded through the window to the corner of the lounge, where Anneke Baas, her hair a tangle of wild filaments, stood on a chair to deliver her daily sermon to no one in particular. Sisters! she was saying. Gather, sisters, that I might quote to you the book that birthed the severed hand, the severed hand torn from the leftmost wrist, an offering of common muscle fed to the mouth, consumed to fuel the body at the right hand's behest. Still we stand knee-deep in the excrement of our own self-consumption. Still we stick to the backmost molars, our flesh against bone, and when the last morsel tumbles into the depths, and its last byproducts are all burnt through, will the right hand have no left hand to prey upon, will the right hand have no offerings left, no means by which to regrow its dominion, no choice but to let itself be consumed... Across the lounge, the other patients sat in silence, staring blankly up at Baas, or at the ceiling, the walls, the floor, hands wringing or feet tapping or lips muttering or all three simultaneously. Anneke carried on and on. Thomas Mertens crossed his eyes, drowsy. Nurse Hendricks smiled to herself as she divvied pills across the cups. Just then, Janice De Groot came in for dayshift. Oh, good, she said. I'm here in time for my favorite part. Mertens spun a circle in his desk chair. Sweet relief! he said. Have fun, ladies. I am going to the pub. And with that he picked up his satchel, clipped on his bicycle helmet, gave three air kisses to each of his colleagues, punched out his timecard and exited the cage to walk the long, subway-tiled hallway where Anneke's voice tailed him up to the exit, the armed double doors he threw wide with ease. It was his Friday, and he was ready for some well-deserved rest.

Acknowledgments

Thanks to the StoneCutters, you foredefeated challengers of oblivion—may you drink responsibly.

Heartfelt thanks to my editor, Caterina Alvarez, for meeting the text where it lives, asking questions of it, and making it all that it could be. Many thanks are also owed to Josh Dale, Kinsey Krachinski, and all the dedicated folks at Thirty West who made this book a reality.

Thanks in particular to those early readers who provided thoughtful and constructive feedback: Benjamin Ficklin, Rick Levin, Michael Steinkirchner, Colin Keating and Bronwynn Dean.

And thanks above all to Kristina, Liam, and Luca, the glowing hearts of my world. For everything. I love you I love you I love you.

About the Author

A.G. Valentine is a writer and multi-instrumentalist from the Pacific Northwest. Throughout an eight-year journalism and freelance career, Valentine published hundreds of articles, mostly about music and food. His words have appeared in several short-run collaborative chapbooks, an array of print magazines and online publications, and the liner notes to one vinyl record.

THE APOPTOTIC ERA is his debut novella.

About the Publisher

Escape the Mundane

Est. 2015

Follow us on:

Scan the QR code to visit.

www.thirtywestph.com